(

Prototype, 26 May 2021, Fiction
Extent: 112 × 178mm, pp.200
Cover: off-white uncoated board
Finish: drawing by Catrin Morgan & typography in black foil
Interior paper: 80gsm off-white uncoated
Print: black offset lithography

Oli Hazzard is the author of three books of poems, *Between Two Windows* (Carcanet, 2012), *Blotter* (Carcanet, 2018) and *Progress: Real and Imagined* (SPAM Press, 2020), and a book of literary criticism, *John Ashbery and Anglo-American Exchange: The Minor Eras* (Oxford University Press, 2018). He lives in Glasgow, and teaches at the University of St Andrews.

Lorem Ipsum
Oli Hazzard

Lorem Ipsum

How foolish I feel when I realise that I have spent another day in front of my inkstone, jotting down aimless thoughts as they occurred to me, all because I was bored and had nothing better to do.
    Yoshida Kenkō, *Essays in Idleness*

Is love when you don't give a name to the identity of things?
    Clarice Lispector, *The Passion According to G.H.*

My mother forgot my son's name, and as she searched her memory for it, while we were on the phone, as I walked slowly around the Meadows, in the freezing air, I found myself thinking of my first day on the Internet, that day so long ago, when I didn't even know what the Internet was, though we had a computer at home, with a number of games on floppy disk, as well as a CD-Rom encyclopaedia which, when I was accepted to grammar school, my mother compelled me to use one day during the summer holidays for research on an 'independent essay' she was going to make me write, since I was going to grammar school, on Ancient Egypt, or perhaps just the pyramids, a prospect by which I was both excited—I liked the idea of knowing about Egypt in theory, of being someone who could recite facts about pyramids, the geometrical calculations which made their assembly possible, the symbolic relation between the structure and the environment, the materials used to construct them and the modes of transport used to move such vast quantities of whatever material (my essay was largely a copy-and-paste job) from somewhere far down the Nile all the way to Cairo, though I think I was also slightly fearful of the possibilities such knowledge could foreclose, such as the possibility that the pyramids had been constructed by aliens, which seemed like an appealing idea, not just, that is, the idea that aliens had built them, but that all this highly advanced activity, this impossible technological feat involving, I imagined, lasers and hovering craft as well as Pharaohs and slaves and whips and ropes, had happened thousands of years ago, and that what we thought of as the past was in fact in many senses already the future (an idea which was also responsible for what was so appealing about the universe of *Star Wars*, it had a dizzying, reversing effect on history, in the sense that it suggested the undiscovered zones of the past might be shown to hold as many interesting things as the future undoubtably did)—and bored in advance, since it would require lots of sitting inside on a sunny day, looking at a screen (as I have been, here, in this small room, writing this to you, A, though with what intention I'm not yet entirely sure) with which I had already begun to self-manage my contact while playing the football game *Fifa 95* (which I often think of as my first 'training' in some of the principles of selfhood to which 'modern literature' would later introduce me, that is, that the 'I' is a fiction, that the unitary self, drawn from the idea of the soul, has long been 'scattered to the wind', that we all contain multitudes and that *je est un autre*, these all felt oddly familiar on first encounter, in part because I had spent months of my childhood, cumulatively, controlling a team of eleven players, each with their own qualities and flaws, rated helpfully in the 'team selection' interface according to category, such as speed, shooting power and accuracy, heading ability, strength and fitness, and when I played a game with my team ('Britain', I think it was, unless I am mistaken, since there is of course no British football team, football remains the domain of individual nations, unlike other areas of life where the category of Britishness comes into play, such as at the Olympics, or on television, or in culture, artists are described as British, sometimes, or writers are British, which seems to me not a helpful designation, since in a loose, semi-formulated way I feel like national imaginaries have more weight and history, or at least more imaginative purchase, than the vague federal category of 'Britain'—Englishness and Scottishness are not synonymous, we know this, but once you've decided on that I suppose the question soon becomes how much specificity can you handle, if you are constantly dividing and subdividing groups of people until they are only named individually, how after all do you make a community (there's that phrase, 'negative community', floating up into my head from something I read at some point in the relatively recent past, where is that from, B, is it, I can't remember, I was probably only half paying attention to the book I was reading at the time, which is more than I usually pay, sometimes when I'm trying to make the best of this chronic inability to focus on a task I think of reading a book—or, rather, *not reading* in the presence of a book—as an opportunity for a bit of daydreaming, sometimes I'll sit myself down in my comfortable middle-class flat in a central area of Edinburgh, with the sound of traffic from the busy arterial road outside dilating and contracting every few seconds, and open something I find really difficult to understand, like some C, and so well-trained have I become at activating in the presence of such texts the trance-like state of a daydream that I only have to read a few sentences, or bump my eyes against the words *hegemony* or *praxis* before I feel my brain evaporating and in its place a bubble of perfect, bland transparency taking up residence, a bobbing, jellyfish-like ambience, through which a gentle, pulsing, roaming form of inattention is enabled, guided less by a desire for escape into a particular other world than by a nosing, blind-feeling, burrowing aversion to the *facticity* of this one—somehow the vocabulary of the unread reading material nevertheless burrows its way into my own—and this experience, if it is an experience, has a syntactical quality to it which feels empty, and luxurious, has a winding, self-delighting, purposeless character, as though everything were suddenly available yet nothing could be retained, which is why when it happens I sometimes find myself saying to myself, dully, self-consciously, 'I am like a work of art right now', or sometimes 'I'm like an object', or sometimes 'I'm a thing' (I feel embarrassed to write these things to you, A, even though I am inventing your presence), and I feel myself reaching out with my newfound mobile jellyfish consciousness to the other things in the room—the sofa I'm sat on right now (long and low, covered in blue velvet, streaked with my son's snot), the coffee table with the broken leg I've been promising to fix since I broke it maybe

a year ago (will this ever happen, probably
mirror set too high in the wall for me to see a..
but the top of my head, books, arranged roughly
according to genre, rug, carpet, lamp, curtains,
television, laptop, phone, complex, mysterious and
low-level menacing thing, arriving fully-formed out
of a set of processes I literally cannot imagine, assembled by machines operated at whatever spatial or
temporal remove by the eyes and hands and brains of
people I cannot see, not just in the sense that I cannot
visualise their bodies at work doing this thing that
they are doing—they are doing it but I cannot see
what it is, this activity from which a phone eventually
emerges—but I cannot imagine their interior lives
as they build this thing my hand rests upon, not an
overly alarming empathetic impasse maybe, since
I basically cannot imagine my own, my own *interior
life*, that is, I often use the word 'interior' without
even momentarily considering what I mean by it,
though I suppose I mean my experience of consciousness, of perceiving and thinking (if that's even
what I do, sometimes it seems like I go for hours
without a single bit of language registering in my
mind, especially when I'm doing something intensely
absorbing and monotonous, like playing *Fifa 2013*
on my PlayStation, which for a long time before our
son was born I would do routinely, once a week, for
four or five hours at a time, and during which sessions
I would enter a kind of trance that was more like being
deeply stoned or experiencing the sensation of a

head drawn out over a drastically
(like that performance piece by D,
seen but feel like I've experienced
times, in which two figures move
ther across a stage at such a glacial
hours pass before their bodies
touch) that is a purposeful meditative state, in the
sense that when I finished playing, and got up from
the sofa and went to the bathroom and looked at my
face in the mirror my eyes were bloodshot (as though
the zoom was up to 150%) and my skin was pale and
I felt like basic sensory phenomena—the cold of the
toilet seat against the tips of my fingers, the sensation
of piss struggling through my urethra down my penis
and out of the too-small slit at the end (when I piss in
such states I sometimes think of my penis as screaming or being sick, and am not unmoved), the low
note of non-communicative noise I emit as this process occurs, which is expressive of neither pleasure
nor displeasure but is simply a noise of *release*—have
to travel through an additional layer of accreted sediment in order to reach that part of my interior that
is alerted to their happening, and I feel like I am
emerging from something distinct from sleep or distraction, a state of having been *away from language*
for a while, and returning from the place where I
had been—a place in which I 'thought' in football,
in the sense that the movements of the players I was
controlling were expressive of 'thoughts' (or maybe
'ideas') which I would otherwise only ever become

aware of if they were articulated in words—is frightening, partly because it makes me realise how smoothly and soundlessly language can fall away, it offers a glimpse of what it might mean to experience that falling away without the subsequent process of retrieval, of having come back from some kind of brink, which has been happening recently to my mother, she has been away from other people for a long time, forgetting words and memories and future events, living alone (I think about her most, and feel closest to her, in fact, when I am alone—aloneness is her element), watching a lot of television, with which she seems increasingly involved emotionally and on which she seems to depend for companionship, particularly programs like *Frasier*—a sitcom designed to be screened in the evening but which because of its age is now shown in two-or-three-episode clusters early in the morning on Channel 4, which results, for me at least, in a strangely and gently disorientating alteration in mood schedule—which is a beautiful program, and its protagonist seems even to me very much like a friend, in fact so much so that I found it weird to listen to the E's episode of *Desert Island Discs* recently and hear him choosing all these cheesy rock tracks and telling these jocky stories, I found it nearly unbelievable—though I didn't think it at the time in words, but more as a general, hovering cloud of potential impressions—that this man could have said literally every word F has ever said without being more substantially affected by that experience, the experience of being spoken through by this character who I think my mother is in love with in a light, leisurely fashion, when I call her in the mornings sometimes she is watching *Frasier* as she speaks to me (she only sometimes turns the sound off) and she tells me she is watching *Frasier* in such a tone of fondness it as if F were literally there in the room with her, *oh, F, he makes me laugh*, a habit which makes it difficult to tell if the long pauses that occur fairly frequently in her conversation are a result of a bad line or a neurological deterioration or if she's just really into the episode that's on), though I think that when I use the word 'interior' what I'm mostly thinking of is dreams, which seem the most deeply interior part of us partly because access to them cannot be willed, and partly because there's something about them which is almost impersonal—we aren't really present in our dreams in any way comparable to how we are present in waking life, since when we are dropped into the unvarying *in medeas res* of dreaming, or at least when I am, I feel as if all my self-consciousness, my understanding of the degree of control I have over my relationship with my environment and how I interact with it, that armour of distance, deixis, has evaporated, and as a result I find myself in my dreams to be completely absorbed by what is taking place, as though I had stepped into the cartoon landscape of *Mary Poppins* (and in doing so, changed into cartoon form myself, though of course that's not what happens to G) or a computer game or another element entirely, with a distinct set of physical laws to which I am totally vulnerable, an exposing feeling of immanence which at once recalls that feeling of being immersed and disorientated in and by the world which is particular to childhood, a feeling which is so intimate it is almost painful to recall and to observe, but at the same time is also a strangely objective-feeling experience, too, as if the substance of dreams, their essentially neutral core, were in fact not much at all to do with me but predominantly external, the enclosed activity of a world only minimally inflected by the sensibility of an individual subject—and there's also the feeling that the word *interior* has something to do with embarrassment, a feeling which is somehow mapped out in the progression of vowels and consonants which constitute the word, one travels *in* to the interior, which in-ness is followed by a blurred or slurred *ter*, which transitions into the complex and laboured and, in isolation, vaguely comic *ior*, which through its conjuring of 'ear' demonstrates an alarming self-consciousness—*the word has seen you listening to it*—and also brings into view the labyrinthine structure of the ear canal, the roots of which extend deep into the dark bodily interior, down towards the throat, which I woke up reaching for last night as I dreamt, as I often do, that our home had been invaded by a man, who had somehow secured the right to use all of the shelves in our flat as display surfaces for the various types of domestic ornament he had for sale, snow globes and statuettes, pet rocks, candle-holders, vases and picture-frames, all of which were crammed onto the shelves (which still supported all of our everyday objects, books and plants and so on, though they, in their new cluttered and crowded accommodation, gave off a distinctly 'harassed' vibe), and when I emerged from our bedroom to question the man about his activity he addressed me with an air of such authoritative irritation—*of course I can, don't you know what time it is*—I deferentially retreated to the bedroom to explain to H that, in fact, the man did have the proper permissions and that there was nothing we could do, a dream drawn straightforwardly and with distortions of only minimal inventiveness from life, since a couple of days previously the buzzer to our flat had gone, and I had buzzed in what turned out to be two policemen, one of whom, in the process of ascending the stairs, called up to me in a tone of authoritative irritation, *don't worry, it's nothing to do with you*, at which statement I deferentially retreated without responding from the communal space of the stairwell to the supposedly private space of my own hallway, back into the living room, where, when I reported this non-exchange to H, she stared at me for a moment, taken aback by the ease with which the words of a person in authority had guided me without objection away from the public space which I had every right to occupy back into our private home, I can see in such instances a flicker of anxiety cross her face, generated, I suspect, by the thought that one

day a man may intrude into our home and I may
be incapable of doing anything about it, a possibility
of which I've often been afraid myself—though at
this stage of our marriage I'm uncertain which of my
uncertainties about myself originated from my own
assessment of my behaviour and interior life, and
which are internalisations of H's own doubts about
me, a strange, ambivalent feeling, not particular
to marriage but perhaps rendered more clearly perceptible by marriage, this knowledge of my own
self-perceptions having become so braided to another
person's perceptions of me that the two are now
indistinguishable, which is, if I'm not mistaken,
something like what I is suggesting in 'Lyric Poetry
and Society' (open, skim-read—and when I say
'skim-read' I really mean something more like 'hover-read', or something, since what I seem to do when
reading this kind of tricky text is pitch my visual
focus at some point just before the text becomes fully
sharpened and legible and wait for what seem like
key words to rise out of the block into a kind of relief,
then from these co-ordinates I'll start to develop a
vague, imperfect conception of the writing's hovering
'concerns' or themes, essentially as if I'm looking at
a map of a terrain or a painting of a landscape, which
we don't process in a linear way, generally, we dot
around from one aspect of the visual field to another
without a conception of 'beginning' or 'end' being imposed, which is what I like about looking at paintings,
this sense of their narrative indefiniteness, an effect

generated, paradoxically, by their staticness, their immobility, an immobility which seems to me to be generous or enabling, because it can act as a stationary point for a registration of surrounding change, that is, the environment in which the painting is encountered (J is good on this), certain paintings I've seen have acquired the status of a time-stamp on the days on which I saw them, and as such carry with them an atmosphere often severely at odds with the one intended by the work, such as K's *Progress: Real and Imagined*, which I saw one very hot day in 2014 at the New Museum in New York, and which depicts a figure at sea, in a boat which is actually a house, open to the stormy elements, and the figure is surrounded by all of the detritus of living and creating things —notebooks, cut-out pictures, photographs, painting equipment and so on—which is a very blustery painting, almost cartoonishly windswept and chaotic (though in the right-hand area the painting opens out, mysteriously and with a surprising fluency, into what seems like another dimension, another aesthetic, through a poster of a winter scene painted from a distance, almost like a memory-bubble extending from the central figure's head) and yet this largely cold and damp scene is for me charged with the intense vertical heat of a June day in New York, when the heat seems to be less an atmospheric condition than a substance, like honey, in which the city is suspended—next to me on the sofa), except, and here I'm almost certainly mistaken, that L is arguing against the idea of there ever being any original interior sensibility separate from the external society in which it's situated), it's a problem that keeps coming up when I teach, my students shake their heads after reading 'The Lake Isle of Innisfree' and say no, this fetishisation of the individual, of isolation, of 'freedom from', this is not the way, but then there's the homogenising effect of globalisation, which we're experiencing today and which makes the social changes which precipitated Modernism seem by comparison local and solvable, and that's no good either, so which is it, and does compromise just make everyone unhappy, and so on—though I am of course aware of the dangers of the nation as a unit of identity, though it seems a disorientatingly changeable idea, as though context were everything and content were nothing, not least since during the first Scottish referendum campaign—I say 'first' because at the moment I'm writing (March 28th 2017, 11:01, on the train to Glasgow, a grey, misty day) it seems likely that a second will be called, since, in M's words, a 'material change in circumstances' was brought about by Britain largely voting to leave the EU, though of course a second one may not come about at all, N may persuade the SNP that 'now is not the time', in that tone she has which makes me wince even to overhear, you can't help but feel it will be directed towards you some day, in the way you have directed it towards your own child, 'now is not the time', you don't know what the time is, the time in history or the afternoon in which we are placed, you must learn more and develop a wider sense of perspective in order to see what has happened and obtain the visionary power necessary to see what is always coming rapidly into view, though of course nobody can ever see beyond what has just come into view, no one is ahead of his time, as O, who wrote like a child, writes, it is only that the particular variety of creating his time is the one that his contemporaries who also are creating their own time refuse to accept, last week I would have assumed that I would know by now whether it is right to say 'first Scottish referendum' or just 'the Scottish referendum'—it would have been odd for those who knew the First World War by its first name of the Great War to later discover that it had been re-named, that it was only the first in a sequence of comparable, numbered conflicts (though, I google, some people appear to believe that the name was given prior to the occurrence of a second war, and that the epithet 'First' was given by a general on the British side who described it in an anticipatory way as 'the FIRST world war' in a projected sequence of future world conflicts)—but because of the terrorist attack on Westminster Bridge and Parliament (I was in fact on the toilet, having a shit, in our flat on Easter Road, when I saw this news on the *Guardian* website, and genuinely did call out to H to tell her something had happened and that she should check her phone, and this after having written what I did below or earlier about that being basically the only eventuality in which having a smartphone seemed necessary, and I felt a bit appalled by my writing it, and then while feeling the feeling I described or describe of the event's insufficiency I also perceived with intense, oxygenating clarity the triviality of my writing, its refusal to really think about what it was saying, I was very harsh on myself for half an hour, and I watched the news live on the television (with the furious concentration of someone intent on changing their life), which I rarely do—we normally watch it on +1, since H gets home from work late and by the time I've put our son to bed I've missed the beginning, and while I know I could simply 'pause' the live transmission I prefer to experience the sensation of watching something according to the rhythms of an invisible, collective audience, even if it is slightly delayed—and it was shocking, initially, what had happened, the terrible deaths of people being run over by a car and a policeman being stabbed to death, and my heart rate went up as I heard it being described—there was no footage, perhaps because the events hadn't been filmed or because there was footage but the television networks had decided against showing it, perhaps it was too shocking or gruesome or they wanted to avoid somehow glamourising or glorifying the act of the individual—this increasingly seems to be the policy among mainstream news outlets, and as I say this I realise that I haven't even seen the face of the Las Vegas shooter, or the Manchester suicide bomber, or the former marine who yesterday murdered twenty-six people in a Texan church, I'm not sure how I feel about that, it's not that I need an image to pin my feelings about these events to, but the absence of an image of a person responsible for these killings feels counterproductive in some respect, it's almost like these figures have been relegated or, in fact, promoted to the status of something invisible or supernatural, and what's frightening about that iconoclastic gesture is that it carries with it the implied reasoning behind iconoclasm when it's intended as an act of reverence—that is, when it's considered an affront to the ideal a deity represents to render its image with the fallen materials of our corrupted world—and so the lack of images of the men who committed these crimes transports them from the material world to the realm of the numinous, amplifying their capacity to 'terrorise' the imagination, though as I write that I feel unconvinced by it, and suspect that what I am really unsettled by is the absence of a head that proves the person is dead, the way, after someone was beheaded, in the eras when this manner of execution was considered permissible (I touch my own head at the thought that this could ever have been the case, and struggle to imagine myself into the mind of someone—P, for example —who would go to an execution as a form of leisure, or distraction, and also purposefully as a way of marking historical moments ('I went out to my Lord's in the morning, where I met with Q [signatory to the death warrant of R] but my Lord not being up

I went out to Charing Cross, to see S hanged, drawn, and quartered, which was done there, he looking as cheerful as any man could do in that condition'), or the minds of those who would then openly take pleasure in the public torture of another person ('he was presently cut down, and his head and heart shown to the people, at which there was great shouts of joy'), though in certain parts of the world this still happens—I remember seeing the image of T on the front page of the *New York Times*, the day we went to the U exhibition, the photograph taken in the moments before his execution, with his executioner standing at his shoulder, and wondering, bizarrely I accept, what I had been doing at the exact instant the image was created—and when it does happen a common reaction is to displace the act temporally, to describe those who carry it out as 'medieval', as though 'modernity' were not itself more brutal than earlier eras) the head would be held up by the hair to the gathered crowd so that they could confirm that this person, convicted of whatever terrible or innocuous or fictional crime, was in fact truly dead and could no longer inflict harm upon the world—I confess I don't know if that would be the right editorial decision—but as the evening went on my heart rate decreased, the streetlights outside began to turn on, and I gradually became aware that I was slowly growing uninterested in the coverage, as it began to dawn on commentators and reporters that this was in fact an isolated incident carried out by an individual rather than the first part of some larger plot, which would have been more exciting and sustaining, in some respects, it's always exciting even if at the same time horrifying to have the veil on the world pulled away a little, as V puts it, and indeed some of the reporters could hardly contain their own sense of disappointment, a feeling which was visible on their faces) the decision about whether to hold a second referendum was postponed, and I'm not sure when it's been rescheduled for—the idea of 'Britishness' was presented 'in some quarters' as an antidote to nationalism, as though Britain as a concept had somehow transcended the bounds of the nation-state and was a form of advance upon the petty or narrow concept of identity drawn from geography, language, history, culture and ideology that nationalism represents (I vaguely remember that sentence from a textbook), and yet, as H said this morning, looking up tiredly from her phone, while the baby napped, when the telescope turned around on itself, in the direction of Europe, Britishness suddenly became a distinct national identity which had to be defined by opposition with the rest of Europe, *what a fucking joke*) I was able to imagine my own selfhood as more-or-less-evenly distributed among those eleven cartoon figures, one of which I would be directly controlling at any one time with the arrow keys and space bar, and the others would be moving automatically in response to that momentarily central figure —and I think even as I was playing then I intuited some relation between that pragmatic, necessary automation of some extraneous parts of the self so that whatever function was being focused on could be performed at optimum level, even as I played I would pick up a glass of water and take a sip or bite from the apple next to the keyboard or continue breathing in and out without giving it a single thought just so that I could score a goal for Britain) since my eyes started to dry and itch after several hours of constant play, a series or compound of feelings, the bored and the excited, I think I anticipated as I sat in the internet café with my mother, looking at a search engine (Ask Jeeves, I think, though that may not have existed in 1997) as though for the first and last time, and unable to remember anything I was interested in or think of anything to write, *though I continued to write anyway*, as W writes in his zuihitsu (the term for a genre, or perhaps antigenre, of Japanese prose writing, which came into being with the composition of *The Pillow Book* (a text which X, a minor courtier during the Heian period, wrote without planning or structure, largely for her own entertainment and 'without thought' for a readership, though she by her own admission only wrote of things which a hypothetical, fictive reader—presumably one much like herself—might find interesting or amusing, including anecdotes, gossip, homilies and pronouncements of taste, lists of interesting and disgusting things and what might in journalistic jargon be called 'opinion pieces'), during the 990s and early 1000s, examples of which are still being written today, even though nobody can agree upon what exactly a zuihitsu is (it seems that it might be the very inability of ten centuries of literary cultures in Japan to successfully and precisely define the boundaries of the genre—its synonyms include 'essay', which evokes the Western essayistic tradition of Y, Z, and B, and 'miscellany', since the constituent elements of the zuihitsu are so often drawn from a range of different subgenres placed alongside one another without any effort to normalise or explain or provide a logic for their relation—is the reason for its endurance, one much-repeated trope in accounts of attempts to write zuihitsu is that in the very attempt to write a successful one the writer renders success impossible, since the parameters of success are somehow both virtual and constantly in motion, and so it is only through an embrace of failure, a pragmatic acknowledgment of the necessity of not adhering to these unwritten rules which are constantly mutating, that one successfully writes a zuihitsu, which is to say that the only way of revering the genre is by treating it irreverently, violating it in such a way that it is left intact, which is the sort of argument that C makes in his essay on literary history and modernity—which I only think of because I was teaching it this morning, tired and hungover and freshly confused by his writing —that is, that the perpetuation of literary history depends upon the rejection of it, is that right, I already can't remember)) *Hojiki*, a short series of reflections upon houses written from his ten-square-feet hut in the province of Kyoto, which features dozens of accounts of natural and man-made disasters which occurred during his lifetime, opening with an epic description of large swathes of the capital city being destroyed by fire ('it was said,' he writes, 'the fire started in Higuchi Tominokoji, and began in a lodging house where some dancers were staying'—the significance of these dancers is not expanded upon —'the flames spread hither and yon on the fickle wind, fanning out wide over the city', he continues, in the translation I have here, expanding the frame of the description in vividly archaic language, 'houses beyond were choked with smoke, while from those nearby, flames spotted and sparks rained down, clouds of ash poured up into the sky, lit red by the fire beneath, and in the midst of all this blazing scarlet the ragged flames leapt whole blocks at a time, flying unresisted on the wind') which appears to be included primarily as a means of dissuading readers from 'building a house in the perilous capital'), a sentence I just had to retype because I was distracted by my son, who, as I write, is sat on the floor next to the table where I sit, reading a book about Peppa Pig upside down, alternating what he appears to think of as 'reading noises' with noises of critical approbation—*oh, ah, ooh*—which is at once distracting and animating, by which I haven't the time to say what I mean since now what's happening is that I'm trying to read aloud the upside-down text of the

Peppa Pig book from a distance of about eight feet, an almost physically painful task, like trying to write with your non-dominant hand, an experience of internal complexity which through its very difficulty (why is difficulty so memorable, and how different is it from pain, return to this if you have space or time) transports me back to the earliest moments of knowledge acquisition in my life, specifically one afternoon when I was a child learning to read in a classroom, conscious of my only partial understanding of the text and images before me, I found myself looking *very hard* at the shapes of the words on the page I was looking at (something about a dog, I remember, because the d had ears and the g had a tail) in order to decipher their meaning, before realising, in some way too immediate to be formulated, that I was in fact looking *too closely* at these words for them to become legible, that what was required by reading was in fact a carefully-managed state of absent-mindedness, a studied form of inattention, which allows us to infer meaning from the sketchiest of familiar outlines at speed, but at this point I'm not sure if what I'm doing is actually reading this Peppa text or simply remembering it with the aid of an incompletely-registered prompt (I have read this story—which is not so much a story as an elliptical account of different aspects of the character of Peppa's mother—so many times it's now possible for me to read it while paying little or no attention to the act of reading, while I'm reading it I can even listen to the radio playing in the kitchen, or think about something that happened to me yesterday, and it's as if my speaking voice has taken on the status of some external, easily ignorable phenomenon, has been absorbed into the category of 'noise', like the constant shushing and parping of traffic from Easter Road outside my window), I sometimes suggest that my students do something similar, that is, I ask them to read the poems I set them sideways or upside down, in order, I say, to slow down the process of reading, to pay attention to the material qualities of the language, in order to de-automate the process of perception, and so on, in this and other ways more or less effective I exert myself to show them that a work of art can still be powerful or moving, it's tiring, performing for them in that way, not least because it feels more often than not counterproductive, that is, my own performance of enthusiasm or scepticism leaves them too little room for their own enthusiasm or scepticism, necessarily distinct from my own, to develop, though it is a particular, privileged-feeling kind of tiredness, unlike the tiredness of my father-in-law, D, who wakes before 6 every morning to work a twelve-hour day in the factory he has run for thirty-odd years, his tiredness is physical, you can see it in the way he moves about a room, and you can tell from his movements that the environment he works in is dangerous, that there is machinery which if you were careless would take a finger or a whole hand off, which is maybe why when he sets the dinner table his movements are very precise, the knives and the forks and the glasses are placed quite exactly, but not pedantically so, he is aware that all physical being in the world is a performance and consequently in some sense didactic, particularly when you're around your own children and grandchildren, and his generosity is not to imply that his precision is the correct way to do something, sometimes he's deliberately a little careless to show that he's not judging those of us who are less exact than he is, that he recognises we all have our own way of going about things, and this care is visible even in his exhausted-seeming body whose exhaustion is quite unlike my own, which is the brittle, weightless kind produced by too little sleep and looking too much at a screen, though only we can know the feeling and extent of our own fatigue, there is no absolute standard, every body is different and some are more capable of enduring work than others, sometimes I feel like my parents (or their generation in the abstract) would be ashamed to see how little work I do, a few hours scattered throughout the day at home, moving from room to room with a fresh hot beverage, checking the news, listening to music, talking to myself in funny voices, playing with our son, this is not a working life they would recognise, me sat here, alone for long stretches, in this tiny cupboard we have converted into an office, pretending to write this to you, A, partly as a byproduct of my reluctance to do any work of instrumental value or pressing need, doodling in

the margins of my actual working life, which is
mainly constituted of emails and marking student
papers, with the very occasional journey to Glasgow
for a day of teaching, though I'm oddly reassured
—and oddly in need of reassurance—even in the
seclusion of my tiny office cupboard, that *visually*
this nevertheless resembles the kind of text which
could be mistakable for work, were someone to look
over my shoulder (*who is looking over my shoulder*,
I sometimes say to myself, in a high-pitched whisper),
and in this sense reminds me of a *contrafactum*—
originally, a musical setting of the mass or a chorale
or hymn produced by replacing the text of a secular
song with religious poetry (New Latin contrafactum,
from Medieval Latin, neuter of contrafactus, past
participle of contrafacere, to counterfeit (translation
of Middle French *contrefaire*), from Latin contra
+ facere, to do) but more commonly today a parodic
or fond or random attachment of new words to
an existing melody, such as when H and I give our
son a bath and we sing, in a highly animated way, the
words *bath time / bathing together / bath time /
everybody loves bath time* to the melody of the theme
song from the series *Hang Time*—an American
teen sitcom centred on the exploits of the Deering
Tornados boys' varsity basketball team in the fictional
Midwestern town of Deering, Indiana, and which
takes its name from a sports term referring to the
length of time that a basketball player spends in the
air—or the singing by members of the Labour party's

Momentum movement the line 'Oh, E' to the tune of 'Seven Nation Army' by The White Stripes, a contrafactum which displays no major conceptual or metrical tension between the original source and the later iteration, whereas the attempt by a small number of Conservative party activists to create a rejoinder with the same melody led to the contrafactum 'Oh, F' which in its bathetic failure to map metrically onto the melody expressed inadvertantly (or, perhaps, purposefully) the inability or disinclination of contemporary conservatives to access even the most basic rhythms of collective speech, a formal failure which is surely expressive of a larger ideological resistance—but which remains essentially something to play with until, say 5pm—though, since fewer and fewer people work according to the fixed working day of previous generations, 5pm itself seems like a dated concept, to misquote G, since we are more likely to wake in the night to check the object next to us that has just buzzed, to check it while watching television next to our spouse or partner or pet or child, to check it on the toilet as we shit in the morning before really waking up, it's crazy, this way of working which isn't even work most of the time, I don't know why I can't stop it since it gives me no pleasure, or even when it serves its function, which I think of vaguely as the reception of information, even on the rare occasions when it does that successfully, as, for example, when my mother has forgotten where she lives, and I use Google Maps to direct her home through the streets of Bristol, or when a terrorist attack occurs, and I find myself grateful for the object because I can rush to tell H that a terrorist attack has occurred almost as it happens, and the telling is if not exactly pleasurable then charged with preternatural urgency because it is the telling of a story which is yet to be resolved, it's like (I say, sketchily, tiredly, to H while we are having breakfast) the experience of reading a great poem, it offers a kind of presentness in the presence of history which feels somehow exhilarating and deflating at the same time, as I suggests, since it never or rarely moves at the pace at which you hoped it would, and even when you are inside the moment of an event, an attack 'unfolding' before your eyes on television, there is an anxious feeling because you are inside the experience which all the previous moments of contentless anticipation were squandered in the service of, and it's not enough, there's something missing, a feeling or phrase or some further escalation of the event which would really secure the experience as historical, which is maybe why I have the object in my hand every morning, to allow for the possibility that I might be shitting historically (H makes a short non-committal *hmm* noise, as she feeds our son avocado mush), and of course, it later becomes clear or is already immediately clear in the moment that on these rare occasions the information could have waited until some point later in the day or until the following morning or forever, which happened when my son was born (I wrote this a few months ago when we only had one child, but since then our daughter has been born, and she is now asleep in our bedroom, the room next to the one I am currently sat in, at 21.17 on Monday 15th January 2018, Blue Monday, so-called because it's the day of the year when people are at their most depressed, an idea which in principle I can get behind—a collective acknowledgement of unhappiness seems to me as likely a cure for unhappiness as anything else—but which is in its realisation disappointing, since despite its location in the year seemingly being determined by a low-point in the social rhythm of shopping for public holidays (the slump between Christmas and Valentines Day) it (what is 'it') nevertheless seeks to convert this reprieve from the obligation to feel happy (sometimes, especially when I'm unhappy, or when I feel like I'm unhappy, or I'm certainly not happy, or feel like I may not be happy—this is a difficult state to properly define, since in some sense, and in some circumstances, happiness and unhappiness seem synonymous —I experience a feeling of clarity which, if not exactly pleasurable, then at least comes as a relief, as a strange and not unwelcome ventilation of my perceptive equipment, my dull body, which I sometimes even seek out, I think, by creating unhappy situations for myself, such as when I argue with my mother unnecessarily by blowing some trivial thing all out of proportion, which makes me wonder if I even want to be happy at all, in the sense that the orders of experience classified under that term (and I say 'classified' only cautiously, since there's not a formal index of these things, though there is a loose, informal, cultural one, of course, which we mentally refer to when responding to new pieces of information, which can be crudely divided into 'happy' and 'unhappy' camps) seem often banal or maybe unexciting or somehow flat-feeling, like having a child, for example, since I just mentioned it, which despite its variable and changing form still seems in some respects like an exercise in emotional homogenisation, which is maybe the point, of course, happiness is presented as a kind of universal experience, when you are happy you will know it—reading this aloud to myself just then, I realised that this morning J, our daughter, who is now ten months old, had clapped her hands as I sang *if you're happy and you know it* to her, which is the first time she has shown any understanding of anything I have said or sung to her, though whether she was responding to the word 'clap', or to the melody of the song, which she has learned to associate with the act of clapping, I don't know—because it is something that everyone can experience, you can plug into the stable feeling of happiness which pre-exists and is somehow exterior to whatever state of unhappiness, or rather non-happiness, in which you found yourself before that moment at which happiness was plugged into or attained, it's as if by entering the experience of happiness you are in fact allowing the experience of happiness to enter you, that is, what is presented in the world (or 'the culture') as the epitome of subjective emotional experience is, in fact, an acute registration of the 'outsideness' or objectivity of feeling, all of which is to say that when we are happy or we desire there is the accompanying suspicion that we are being *felt for*, a possibility which is in itself, I realise, neutral, so maybe it's not even happiness itself which I object to so much as any stable term for a state of feeling, it seems like it would be a better idea for the words we have to describe emotional states (or 'affective states', or whatever more exact term has now supplanted this one, even though I'm still relatively young from some perspectives I'm already starting to feel left behind by the progress of the language, the beginning of a process which will at some future moment surely conclude with my children holding me, at best, in amused contempt, or perhaps that's too strong, depending on how things go with their lives and the lives of everyone around them as time passes, perhaps they will be more tolerant than I am) to be more mobile or dynamic than other words, so that, for example, it could be possible to take all of the letters of all of the dominant emotions, happiness, sadness, anger, jealousy, fear, horror (is that an emotion), and so on, and break them down into their constituent parts (their letters) so that you could then select the aspects of your happiness best represented by, say, the 'h' and the 'p' and the 'e', then combine that with 'j' of jealousy and the 'f' and 'r' of fear (since of course all happiness is contaminated by, or necessarily dependent on combination with, these other feelings, in varying ratios according to temperament or sensibility of the feeling subject) and whatever synthetic unintelligible word was created through their combination could be employed temporarily to represent that state, and then after it was spoken or written returned to its prior or original state of being merely letters—a pretty stupid idea, and exactly the kind of 'thought-doodle' which when I emerge from it makes me feel most acutely how embarrassed I would be to be observed in this activity, especially by my gardener father or my teacher mother or my journalist and bus-driver grandfathers or my cleaner and nurse grandmothers, this implacably sceptical invisible audience, especially if I were to think of it as any kind of 'work') into another 'opportunity for the purchase of happiness', I only found out that this day existed because Yo Sushi sent H a promotional email stating that today diners would receive one free blue plate if they spent over £10, so we went there for lunch with our daughter in her buggy (our first proper excursion out into the world with her—a small excitement, an electrical charge somewhere beneath the surface of our exhaustion—the unexpected winter sun seeming very bright and harsh, but probably health-giving (she's a little jaundiced) on her fresh, sensitive skin, it seems strange to me and miraculous to have been involved in the creation of something capable of sensual experience in the world, when I see the sun illuminating the detailed terrain of her skin (shapes of non-human-seeming exactness combined with mysterious unaccountable irregularities, field-like patches of fine fair hair, bumps and spots, creases, rhomboid inflammations and little angry eruptions of pus—possibly seborrhoea dermatitis, caused by overproductive oil-producing glands in the skin) and imagine what it must be like to feel that sensation —the sun on your skin—for the first time, the warmth of it soaking through layers of cells deep into the darkness of her interior (weird that our insides will always, or mostly, be dark) I find myself momentarily and melodramatically transferring all faith I have in the ability to experience the world sensuously to her, as though in the process I were abdicating the role of guiding subjectivity in even my own life and assuming the automaton-like subsidiary position of a player (cf. the *Fifa 95* memory above or below) purely reactive, within the scope of certain predetermined parameters, to the live desires of another) but it was full so we left and went elsewhere), during a period of 48 hours or so when H and I stopped using our phones, she because she was in labour, giving birth, then recovering, and I because (I later wrote in the notes section of my phone) *I think I realised that the desire for experience to be potentially historical had evaporated with my son's arrival, and what I now wanted was an experience somehow exempt from history, a kind of enclave or recess or pouch of some kind in time's onward flow, a feeling that was quite unexpected and made his birth and his existence seem all the more potent and powerful*—reading that back it seems a lot, but it's more or less true, it's just about the most reliable indicator of my interest, I'm aware of the desire to look at my phone at all times, and if I'm doing something and I don't feel that desire then I know I must be experiencing high levels of interest in the other thing, it's almost a principle of criticism for me, now, when I read a novel or a poem or an essay, there's an internal pressure gauge constantly straining towards the 'put this down and pick up your phone' end of the spectrum, which as time has gone by has become increasingly sensitive, though I confess I haven't yet got to the stage where I'll put a book down before the end of a page, somehow that formal marker, even though more often than not an arbitrary one determined by the formatting processes of publishers, rather than the greatly more significant marker of the paragraph conclusion, has remained sacred for me, and if I abandon that last vestige of my reading habit I have the feeling that I may never read a book again—*but it*, I continued, *my son's birth, that is, also made me realise that what I had previously wanted in part was a feeling of exposure to danger, to change, and action, and novelty, whereas when K was born I think I felt, genuinely for the first time in my life—and here, of course, my whiteness becomes a factor, though I wonder if my gender is more important, or my money, or education, I don't know, in all likelihood the degree of influence of these factors have on my character and behaviour isn't exactly or even loosely determinable from inside them, so that I wonder if even pointing them out isn't pointless, or even intended as exculpatory or even self-congratulating (look how right I am about my wrongness, etc.)—vulnerable, on behalf of my son but also vulnerable myself because of my confused feelings of love and protectiveness towards and fear for him, so for the first time felt the presence of history as an external pressure, not malign, but indifferent, and physically very powerful, like a wave or hurricane or flood or some other phenomenon of unthinking nature I've never experienced, that blasts and topples and burns and drowns with the blithe, expressionless carelessness of a bored child, and I wanted to opt out, I wanted us to be overlooked, to be spared, to be excepted from the rule, and I didn't want to know, I remember thinking that to myself, I don't want to know, take it away, put it to one side, tell somebody else, not me, not today, not me, I felt the internal gauge still itself, and it felt reactionary, politically, this feeling, though the category of politics had momentarily lost all meaning for me, standing holding my baby looking out from the window of the maternity ward, and this despite the fact that his birth had also been the most intimately political event of my life, I was left speechless by it, stupefied by the whole infrastructure of care for my son's body, for H's body, for me, and just let myself be sped along in it, in a way, paralysed by gratitude for a visible extension of politics that was so all-encompassing as to be invisible, and yet nothing could interest me, nothing could draw my attention away from the alcove of our new life, to such an extent that I started to view the feeling of interest itself as suspicious, when it first returned to me, when I was changing his nappy, in the ward, two days after he was born, and the radio was on, and the news came that dozens of people had been killed in Paris, I felt my interest returning, and yet I felt it as if it were an outside thing, a corrupt feeling, something not coming from within, it's hard to describe, it's hard to describe in a way that makes me feel like a child, unable to control himself or to articulate why, I felt repulsed by my desire to know as if I were watching that desire happen to someone else, and my combination of pleasure and displeasure in watching this other person's combination of pleasure and displeasure generated high levels of anxiety in me, as if I were an infinite cast of slightly modulated but interchangeable versions of the same rough template, and I just couldn't work out how I had ended up exactly like myself, trying to put on this nappy with a degree of carefulness mixed with carelessness to which I had become accustomed as my characteristic approach to the world, particularly when it comes to physical tasks, I can barely put the dishes away without breaking something but, on the other hand, I put a poem or an essay or a work email together as if everything depends on it, nothing is unintended, everything is functional, even the errors and the flaws, the flattery and censure, the discretions and the disclosures, so that reading it is (so I imagine) like walking through a space whose architecture and interiors are not obtrusively designed-feeling, and whose materials are sufficiently various to avoid a feeling of sterility, and it feels right as an aesthetic because this principle of combination is visible everywhere in the external world, so that when I'm wandering around anywhere, really, I am often reminded of that passage in* The Renaissance *in which L describes the transportation of soils from different regions to one place to be combined, Jerusalem, I can't remember it exactly or even inexactly, it seems, but the idea or principle underlies even the space in which I'm writing to you, Richmond International Airport, perched on a stool at a 'Recharge Station', a kind of bar counter made of some wood (I can feel that it is wood by running my finger along the underside) with some plastic material fixed to its top surface displaying a pattern, a mixture of tiny brown, black, white and beige dots, hundreds of which could be fitted onto the nail of my index finger, attached to the wall, beneath a sign (I say 'beneath', though it in fact begins at the level of the counter, level with my lower ribcage, and extends three or so feet above my head) advertising a company called Dominion, depicting a white man of around thirty (which would make him the same age as me, though of course I think he looks like an ancient adult—and needless to say I feel his whiteness is somehow more pronounced than my own, expressed principally by the level of his waistband—though I am coming to the realisation, incrementally, that I am no longer as young as I think I am, I've had students try to explain to me what Facebook is) in a hard hat, holding a laptop, smiling directly at the viewer while an African American man kneels in front of him, his hands twiddling with some knobs and wires in what looks like a data centre, in fact must be, since I have now read the text of the advert, the most interesting claim of which is that 50% of the world's Internet traffic passes through Northern Virginia, and what's interesting and a little vertigo-inducing about that for me right now is not that all that internet passes through Northern Virginia but that I'm struggling to visualise how it 'passes' at all, in what sense does it (what is 'it'?) 'pass' through the metallic shelves that the second figure's hands are touching at just above my eye-level, at which he is smiling in apparent satisfaction, perhaps satisfaction at the high-quality job he is doing (so good, perhaps, that it's worth advertising), or maybe at the simple fact that this is the job he has chosen to do, perhaps he is one of those lucky few who end up doing something with their lives for which they are particularly well-equipped and well-suited, though a part of me doesn't really believe that anyone is more 'suited' for anything than anyone else, or at least hopes that this is true, that biologically we begin more or less equally, though of course some people run faster than others, and others have a facility for music or maths that seems far beyond the norm, and of course some people are employed because of how they look, which is largely beyond their control, like these two men pretending to be internet database workers in North Virginia, or perhaps they are in fact actual workers at Dominion, that kind of 'authentic' advertising (using actual workers in an organisation to encourage us to 'join the team', and so on, advertising as a sub-branch of autofiction, or vice versa) seems increasingly prevalent, though the idea of calling such talents 'natural' seems wrong, for obvious reasons which are still relevant, still, it does feel that life is divided into an infinite number of parallel streams, each progressing at different rates, a fact which is dramatised by the various re-enactments you encounter in this state, as when in Colonial Williamsburg a man running the old post office, dressed in eighteenth-century garb, asked me if I was loyal to the crown, and when I responded by asking him if he was loyal to his president, he refused to acknowledge his existence, not with any particular delight, but rather, in fact, with a kind of flickering wince, a momentary pained expression on his face at my having brought into the foreground against his will a particular condition of his working life, which I now feel guilty about, why couldn't I just let him do his job, even if his job is pretending history since 1765 hasn't happened, imagine how annoying I must have been and how frequently visitors must attempt to get him and his colleagues to break character (as if he were a guard outside Buckingham Palace, which doesn't even have being a re-enactment to recommend it) even as they process the card transactions on their machines, though I wonder how frequently that kind of irreverent challenge does happen, since, in the words of the Uber driver (who, it quickly became clear, had voted for M, mainly because the introduction of Obamacare had obliged him to take up the expensive health insurance*

offered by his own employer, rather than continue as an additional party on his wife's employer's cheaper, superior plan, as he had been for many previous years, but also because of his desire to see his country return to an earlier iteration of itself, the one perfected around 1985, a desire which was communicated only gradually and with some hesitation during the forty-minute drive, partly, I think, because he had initially assumed I was a 'liberal' since he had picked me up from an inn across the street from the College of William & Mary, and also in part because I am English, or British, but when it became clear that I wasn't dogmatically 'liberal', by which I guess he meant left-wing—I had in fact assumed, internally, a position of 'curiosity and openness' towards this man, who was good-humoured and friendly—he tentatively began to explain his frustrations about the present moment and his anxieties about the future, which I cannot currently remember) who dropped me off at the airport, often visitors don't want to have the 'bubble' burst, which is why the handful of people who actually live in the Colonial area are obliged to keep their shutters closed at all times (or perhaps it's only during 'opening hours', I don't know) and so must live in the dark, or rather in the lamp-light, since the last thing you want is to be walking down the street, imagining yourself into the Colonial period and have the misfortune to look in through a rare unshuttered window and see someone watching their flatscreen TV, eating their modern lunch, how irritating that would be, though I wonder if the bubble isn't already at least a little endangered by other, more obvious ruptures in period detail, which leads me to conclude that perhaps it's not so much the fact of anachronism that causes irritation, perhaps even distress (it's my only holiday of the year, I want it to be good and memorable and so on) as that it occurs out of place, out of its element, whereas it's easy to ignore the unignorable card machine in the souvenir shop because there's no contradiction there, you can hardly expect money to dress in period clothes, such a detail doesn't upset or disturb, in fact it comforts, maybe, that there are things of our world that cannot be erased no matter how thorough the re-enactment, even though it sometimes seems like the only thing which would satisfy this desire to experience the past would be to actually enact the past completely by erasing the present altogether, the thinker of this thought included, it's why tourists hate themselves, of course, or if they don't they should, since they ruin the experience they want to experience by their simple presence, I read that somewhere, though I can't tell exactly where, increasingly as time passes all books seem to absorb each other and become agglomerated into one book, while at the same time what was lived and what read have become difficult to distinguish, and the divisions between them are becoming flimsier, more transparent, so that it is possible for the inhabitants (for some reason I'm imagining memories as having become personified) of one of these zones (the read and the lived) to look through the translucent film separating them from the other, presumably larger and more expensively equipped zone and get a look at what's going on, until the desire to reach the other side becomes so powerful that it somehow happens, and a kind of commerce or economy of exchange begins, so that what began as something lived loses a dimension, gets flattened out into something with the texture of something read, and something read takes on the qualities of something lived, it has that same potency and irreducible essence, that mixture of almost vegetal fullness and severity, which we can identify without being able to name when we think of something that happened to us in life, though actually I wonder if this is in fact a novel or recent sensation or one which has been present in some form since the beginning of my reading life, which I've started to recollect more frequently as my son begins to learn to read, as when I read *Middlemarch* on the bus to school and back over a couple of weeks when I was fourteen, much of the time unhappy and afraid of some sudden, random, minor violent act (you could be walking between classes down the series of labyrinthine, fake gothic corridors that extended through the buildings of the grammar school I attended and suddenly you'd experience a deep, dull pain in your thigh, 'a dead leg', from someone having kneed you there, for no reason, it was skilfully exact, an injury pitched expertly just below the threshold of unacceptability) though relieved just about often enough by pockets of pleasure or distraction in sport and literature, my own body and the bodies of my friends, which because of their changing states during adolescence became a subject of intense shared interest, the changes that were happening were common to us all though they rarely if ever happened simultaneously (the parallel timelines of physical development we each embodied connected us to one another, in that they provided us with a shared concern, a common temporality of change and bewilderment we all inhabited and authenticated, but when particularised at the level of the individual they also drove us apart —one of us would, seemingly overnight, grow by a few inches, prompting a reshuffle in the physical hierarchy, or develop a sudden cluster of hair under each arm, or a voice would, all of a sudden, and sometimes in the middle of speaking, seem to break, and the collective nature of our shared time would appear to be ruptured by this individuation, despite the fact that its ongoingness depended on, was in fact constituted of, such individual breaches taking place), we would compare our bodies and the methods by which we explored them and the nature of their secretions in great detail, I remember one long conversation on the bus home from school trying to describe as exactly as we could the smell and taste and texture of come, its peculiar and distinct perfume, salty and fishy, pungent and bland, in appearance nacreous (a word I'd recently picked up from *Lolita*), at once repellant and attractive, strange and synthetic but also somehow basically human-seeming, trying to bring this new substance—whose phenomenal elusiveness seemed to be expressed through the fact that its name was a noun which was also a verb—which we had only recently and involuntarily started to produce into intelligibility together, and these intimate verbal exchanges (usually conducted with an intensely anxious nonchalance, talking too loud) often gave way to less controlled or self-conscious engagements, that is, we were often on the verge of fucking each other without knowing it, and for me the speaking of words is bound up in that half-perceived constant imperfect arousal, I remember in particular one Friday night when four of my closest friends slept in my house (we'd spent the evening skateboarding in the car park of the local Baptist church, then smoking joints in the quarry behind the 1960s estate that had developed around my family's house—a converted barn which, because of its position at the upper limits of housing on the hill, and its striking bright yellow colour, could be seen from across the town, which I always found reassuring, and was a little vain about—and had climbed up through the woods to a vantage point above the quarry, a stone ledge that sloped gradually then steeply towards the edge, thirty feet above the thick overgrowth of brambles and stinging nettles) we were laid out in the dark on the floor of the living room, postponing the descent into sleep which would, as always, only occur after unanimous agreement, as though we were agreeing to enter a shared dream (perhaps influenced by the process of shared dreaming depicted in *The*

Matrix, a 1999 American science fiction action film written and directed by the Ns and produced by O, starring P, Q, R and S, about a dystopian future in which humanity is unknowingly trapped inside a simulated reality, the Matrix, created by intelligent machines to distract humans while using their bodies as an energy source, a film I watched perhaps thirty times as an adolescent, often at sleepovers with my friends, and one of those films which has been irrevocably changed by information subsequently released about the casting choices made during preproduction, such as the fact that the role of Neo, which would ultimately be played by T, was initially offered to U, V, and W (none of whom wanted to take up the role because filming was due to take place in Australia), a set of alternative versions of this character which seem almost impossible to me from this vantage, but when I rewatched the movie recently (it remains excellent) I realised that as I watched I was imagining those other actors in the role they refused, their faces and voices overlaying the face and voice of the actor who actually play the part, what actually happened ghosted or shadowed by what might have happened but never actually did, a chorus of possible variants) and I started describing fucking someone, slowly, and in fantastic detail, in an empty classroom or in the school toilets, I forget, but they seem the most likely locations, a particular girl with whom we were collectively 'obsessed' had become in this scenario suddenly a willing medium for the expression of our desires, and as I described this scenario they were getting hard, they all told me, in a state of comic agony, *I'm getting hard, X* (as I was briefly, ludicrously known), I'm getting hard, both a complaint and an encouragement, and I kept speaking, the scene elaborating itself before me, or rather as if it were somehow embodied in the image of the words themselves as they were projected vaguely 'before' me, it didn't feel as if I was imagining or inventing anything, but simply *calling it forth* from the background into which it was mysteriously coded, distinguishing itself from the uniform substance that everything unarticulated is, like the slowly perceived image in a magic-eye puzzle, and I don't recall how it ended, the story about the fucking—the particulars of which would have been drawn entirely from 10-minute long midnight previews on adult channels, which were essentially a handful of trailers for different hardcore porn films spliced together (I recognise trace effects of this first visual encounter with sex in motion —I had, of course, seen photographs of naked women before this point, in the porn magazines that friends' parents kept in their bedside tables, or contained within those pens which, when turned upside down, gradually uncover the body of the woman suspended in the transparent chamber which forms part of the upper body of the pen, but it seemed to me then that there was a vast difference between static images of sex and moving ones—with my own sexual 'style' in my late teens and early twenties, which was

characterised by my 'cutting away' from one
position or angle to another rapidly, as though the act
of sex itself were a montage of acts, displaced from
elsewhere, presumably to give the impression of over-
riding 'passion' or inventiveness or, at least, energy,
an approach which eventually tested the patience
of one girlfriend to such a degree that she had to tell
me to calm down, to stay in one position, to try to
feel what was happening rather than fucking in such
a way that it gave the impression that I was trying to
arouse the later version of myself who would one day
be recollecting these scenes)—I don't know if they
came, or I stopped, or we laughed, or whatever, but
something had happened to the bodies of others
because of something I'd said, and whether it was a
form of harm I wasn't entirely sure, I remember feeling weird, a mixture of embarrassed and hostile, the
next time I saw the girl whose image I had animated
for my friends' benefit, but even today all (or most)
buses remind me of *Middlemarch* so strongly I
feel like all I have to do is look into my lap and the
book will be there, waiting to be picked up, for the
words, which have been slowly churning around
the page like a storm in the distance seen through a
drawing-room window, to correct themselves into
their proper arrangement, this kind of error of cogni-
tion or flickering, momentary hallucination makes
me think now and again, when I read about such
things, in the work of Y, for example, that in all prob-
ability that moment—the ongoing moment of

reading—is still happening, at some location, and that in some future location that already exists it has become possible to perceive its continual occurrence, or, since 'occurrence' suggests time is dynamic, its permanent installation, as a kind of sculpture (is this why sculpture is the least interesting art form, because there's something overly-literal about it, its truthiness is 'a little on the nose', a phrase I think I heard for the first time and understood only in my early twenties, like 'not to put too fine a point on it', a phrase I first heard spoken by a friend who had changed so drastically since I'd last seen him I could scarcely believe he could keep a straight face, as he walked me to a pub in Oxford (before a poetry reading I was about to give) in a suit and bowtie, swinging and tapping his umbrella, and prefacing some nuanced-but-not-so-nuanced-as-to-seem-pedantic remark with 'not to put too fine a point on it', I was so embarrassed by him and his new set of affectations, and also embarrassed by my envy of the ease with which he wore them, the lack of embarrassment at his disassociation from the person I had known, and I felt the contagion of his desire for change, and in the directness of his gaze he told me he knew I knew how he had changed and that he didn't care, and momentarily I wanted to imitate or somehow acquire that attitude (I am extremely susceptible to other people's personalities, if someone I meet displays a trait which I find charming or interesting or appealing—for example, enjoying gossip even while acknowledging that it's mean, having the ability to talk unabashedly about yourself while suspecting, or even knowing, that you are boring the other person slightly, talking to children as though they were adults, rather than in the sickly, fictional vernacular in which adults usually talk to children, having hobbies or interests that seem entirely unproductive or unrelated to your working life, enjoying the limitations of your own knowledge in certain areas—say, you enjoy the experience of listening to the music of Z in a particularly intense way in part because you are aware that your understanding is limited, partial, or amateurish, and that even though you're well aware there are further, more developed and nuanced forms of understanding of that experience which could be sought out and cultivated, you know you never will seek out or cultivate them, because you are content with your partial understanding, which is a kind of gift to yourself— sustaining eye contact for prolonged periods without shame or embarrassment, having the desire to categorise and systematise knowledge and experience, to come up with theories to explain things in broad terms in order to prepare yourself for the encounter with new experiences in the future, while being ready, and, even, especially pleased, to acknowledge exceptions and anomalies, things that don't fit the model, being imprecise and uncertain in terms of knowing what attracts your attention (which suggests an enviable attitude of openness and generosity, and an appealing sense of doubt about the sources of aesthetic pleasure) while being very exact in understanding what appals and disgusts (it seems to me there's something almost more expressive about what we resist or deny than what we embrace and accept, it provides a more exact image of our sensibility, for example when B lists, in her matter-of-fact way, a small number of 'disgusting things', as she does throughout *The Pillow Book*, she begins with 'the underside of something sewn', which seems very idiosyncratic to me, and immediately gives a sharper image of her personality than any enthusiasm might do—especially since, of course, the thing which disgusts her here seems closely analogous to the kind of writing that she herself is doing, that is, writing with the seams exposed, writing in which she is licensed to express disgust for the medium in which it happens—though her enthusiasms are also expressive in their own way, it is unusual, for example, to find the sound of someone clearing their throat in the morning appealing), finding something potentially personally embarrassing, awkward or exposing funny, and actually laughing at it (not just because the person is comfortable enough in themselves to find themselves amusing when they get something wrong, but because it gives the impression, however distantly or obliquely, that the personality is in itself a social, collectively-authored phenomenon, one which can be constructed and dismantled and repackaged in real time by a person with and through and among their friends and acquaintances and enemies, which, while a basically stressful, stretching idea, also makes everything seem possible), or refusing to enjoy gossip because it's mean, and you know that there are unforeseen social consequences from even the slightest indiscretion or speculation, a ripple in the lattice of things—it doesn't take long, sometimes literally a few seconds, for me to begin imitating it, not, I think, as a way of winning approval ('see how similar we are', etc.) but rather just to try on someone else's personality for a while, their manner of speaking, the position of their body in a chair and perspective on the world, it's involuntary, more or less—though sometimes, when I'm in the mood to view such passivity as weak or pathetic (usually, I confess, in emulation of the mood and view of someone I am talking to), I try to assert my own personality with a series of internal commands before speaking, such as, 'disagree with that statement and articulate that disagreement in a fashion that somehow suggests you're left-handed', and it feels so contrived I find my body language and manner becoming weirdly contrived—and though I used to feel shame about this imitative character trait I no longer do, in fact much of the time it seems to make a lot of sense that your personality should be conditioned by your immediate circumstances more than other factors such as personal history or class or prior preferences or opinions, that it should be a constant improvisation concocted with the materials closest to hand, the thing I read today, the room I'm in, what I had for lunch, and above all who I'm talking to, a way of existing which has its benefits, since I rarely know what my day will be like, I never get too depressed (an uptick in mood is only ever one cheerful person away), the fact that becoming so ha-bituated to change means that you essentially become immune to change (which sounds like a truism but is also true) and, most helpfully, it gives you an unusual insight into people's characters—if someone is used to people imitating them, for example, because they have a particularly winning or interesting personality, then they might be comfortable with and not even register the imitation, an approach I admire and would strive to emulate, though there is often a noticeable drop in interest as they speak to the one imitating them, for often the most unique and interesting people are only truly interested in other unique and interesting people, since it is the quality of particularity or singularity above all others that draws them to one another, and the idea that you would be drawn to others with whom you have 'things in common' is anathema, but on the other hand sometimes such people 'crave' this imitation by others, see themselves as not really existing unless they can detect their own presence in another's speech, in their body, on their face, and others, much more rarely, are repulsed or offended by it, I have seen this on only one or two occasions, once, I remember vividly, when I was speaking to a man with a stutter that I thought was a very beautiful mannerism —the intimacy of the combination of hesitation and

frustration and the overwhelming desire to speak
—I found myself, after only a brief period of easy and
pleasant conversation, suddenly, and against my will,
stuttering over my own words, and as this happened
I saw this man's face change entirely, he looked
shocked and hurt and angry, of course, since it appeared that I was mocking his speech impediment,
how could it be anything else (*it's kind of a compliment*, I wanted to cry), a horrifying realisation which
made my new-found stutter even more acute, and my
blush deeper, it was awful, though, because he was a
tolerant and polite person, he never said anything, we
continued our conversation for a few minutes more,
exchanging stuttered remarks, and he left the bar, and
I was left alone at a table whispering to myself effortlessly the very same words over which I'd struggled
only moments before) the change seeming a 'salutary'
one) though of course I don't believe it, or only
semi-believe it, since duration is the substance of
experience, the *is* of the thing, as C writes in her
novel or essay or diary or monologue (what *is* it?),
Água Viva, I can feel it within and around me as I
type these words while K naps in the back seat of the
car, their sequential release from the vague, lush
space of all possible actions into the austere pristine
hygienic finality of actual events, a continuous or
prolonged present ('In that there was a constant recurring and beginning there was a marked direction
in the direction of being in the present although
naturally I had been accustomed to past present and

future, and why, because the composition forming around me was a prolonged present,' D wrote in her 1925 lecture-poem 'Composition as Explanation' of *Melanthca* (a full-scale reworking of her first book, *Things as They Are*, which was written in 1903 and published posthumously in a limited edition in 1950, the plot has been changed and the central trio reduced by one, but the characters and their motivations, the fatalistic philosophy, and some phrases remain familiar), 'I created then a prolonged present naturally I knew nothing of a continuous present but it came naturally to me to make one, it was simple it was clear to me and nobody knew why it was done like that, I did not myself although naturally to me it was natural,' a sense of the present as an obdurately permanent installation in space, of each moment always happening, and which is only fully inhabited or registered by the process of trying to account for it, through stories that time tells itself to explain its passing, as E puts it, when I think of it it makes me think I'm going to go mad, or at least that a kind of madness seems suddenly like the other option I'm always not taking, at every moment, doing anything but cutting my wrists is a decision in favour of life, but writing it down—this feeling of duration, that is —as it happens feels like the only thing (aside from sex, for which I don't currently have time) capable of filling up the moment with enough to satisfy it, as if the space we experience as time is needy, as though its self-image were dependent on the idea that it can be at once invisible *and* felt by the occupants of its structure, as when I read an essay or a story or a poem I find myself wanting and failing to infer the larger structure of a person from what fragment or residue has been presented to me, which is another critical device, the potency of the hallucination of a person a literary work can generate, the more felt the virtual presence of that impossible person the better the work, I think—though this absurd precept (which is all that's needed for thinking about something to begin, a precept, and whether or not it's true or provable or ethical or funny or repressive is neither here nor there, a further precept which is also merely neutral and enabling) is premised on the more important counter-assumption that to be perceived and named as you actually are is both the ultimate end of all of this activity and the one thing whose realisation would put an end to it all, and as such must be deferred for as long as possible, the trouble being, of course, that the actual self which is finally perceptible (as it is for everyone, we all add up to something in the end, a last tally, however inaccurate or distorted) is made up predominantly of the gestures employed to evade such detection, it reminds me by antithesis of one of the few things I know my father said, *I am an open book*, my mother reported this to me once, I'm not sure why, but I think it was presented as a sign of his quality of character, this willingness to be known, this refusal to evade detection, perhaps it struck my mother as something worth admiring

and something worth reporting to her child since
she was and remains a book constituted of exactly
the kind of anxious and elaborate misdirections I
mentioned just now, a fact I think she was aware of
though not to such an extent that it prevented her
from presenting the 'brittle spectacle' (in F's words)
of a coherent self to the world, to compensate for
which my father was cited in this manner as the ideal
person, repository of all the complimentary and contrasting features in which my mother was deficient,
who in his physical absence could fulfil not only the
role of infinite resource for desired traits but make
possible the dream of being finally knowable, a composite figure of manageable complexity an actual
image of whom could be assembled from the photo
albums piled in their haphazard fashion in the
bookshelves—photographs (as I began writing this
unexpected passage I confess I expected a feeling of
pathos to accompany its composition, arising from
the general fact of my father's death, but then particularising to the more intensely focused sadness of
the fact that my 'visual memory' of him—which
is of course not a memory, since when he died I was
too young to form memories, so what I refer to as a
'visual memory' is in fact a layering of memories of
looking at photographs of events I never experienced,
people I never knew, the repeated encounters with
which have nevertheless over time accreted into
something which has the texture of a memory, a lived
experience—is drawn from such a limited archive

of images, a few dozen, in fact, from an entire life, which seems shocking to me, now, that is, that the visual record of a life can be condensed to a handful of still images, that such a slim record, a thin precipitate, of a life could be left over, when there are single days when my face, in all its various uninteresting and meaningless expressions, is captured hundreds of times, carelessly and even thoughtlessly, by H or my children or the surveillance state, when we play with my iPhone, and they take probably more images of me in a minute than were taken of my father's face during his entire life, an unsettling (if only in the sense that it reveals to me how much I normally equate the gesture of recording with an underlying sense of the value of what is being recorded) thought, but surprising for me in the sense that when I wrote the passage that follows what I experienced was not the anticipated sadness, but rather a kind of nostalgia, nostalgia for the partialness—even the restraint—of the existent record of my father's life, the definiteness with which each singular moment was captured and preserved, and as I was thinking about it, able to hold virtually all of these materials in mind at once as I tried to assemble an impression of this unknowable person, I became less distressed and increasingly grateful for the sheer *manageability* of the amount of information about my father I have to work with, especially in comparison with the task I imagine my own children will have to face, when I eventually die of whatever disease or accident might befall me, and they will have to between them (there are currently two, but maybe we will have more children and the decision-making processes about my collected effects they will have to undertake together will have to be formalised in some way, a kind of committee) decide what to do with the hundreds of thousands of photographs stored in my cloud, or the hundreds of thousands of emails in my inbox, I don't even delete emails from Amazon or whatever, weirdly it's become the default, the easy option, to just *preserve everything*, since, after millennia of it being the case that huge amounts of effort had to be expended in order to preserve archives (I've recently dumped a load of text about the Library at Alexandria into this sentence somewhere, or maybe I deleted it) in the hope of shaping a future conception of the past and determining the shape of the future, today it's a lot more effort *not to archive* than it is to meticulously record, obviously I don't have the time to delete the six variants which exist of every posed photograph I take with my children, which is odd, to think that one day, when I'm dead and they have my passwords, they will encounter a photo in my phone which they will perhaps know (I still get photos printed and put them in frames and dot them about the house, perhaps that gesture is important enough in itself —establishing a 'canon' of authorised images—and makes all this worrying redundant) surrounded by its other iterations, those same faces in those same situations fractionally altered by the minutest intervals of time, each a hand's breadth on from the next, it's hard to know how they would approach it, if they would feel these supplementary photos are discardable, or disposable, or important minor variations, perhaps for the generation my children are part of the sense that the image of the person is somehow sacred or significant will have evaporated completely, and they will have no reservations about junking all of the images, though I wonder where their own expectations of pathos might live—in the fact that unlike their own children they will no longer be able to smell me (since I never got round to storing my body scent in the future archive I'm imagining), or converse with me in the way that their own children will be able to converse with their own artificially stored consciousnesses, or something) in which he only ever wore a series of isolated, unmoving expressions, and as such appeared expressionless (unless you undertook the imaginative exercise of attempting to connect the one face smiling at the child he is holding—me—to the other face staring with what seems like mock-fury directly into the camera, something I have tried but which immediately proved itself beyond me—that motion of turning away from me to the right, the smile in the mouth and eyes loosening or crumbling to an expression of exaggerated blankness, the lips slightly parted, the eyes widened just far enough to convey the non-seriousness of intent, the background changing (slowly, in rough flecks and flakes, as though the scene itself were deciduous) from a dusty yellow street in the height of a Spanish summer to a cool, dark interior, somewhere in a building which probably still stands—since it seemed that it is exactly in the syntax of graduated change between complete or finalised facial expressions that character, or soul, or spirit, or sense, or whatever it is that we want to call it (what is 'it') for the time being is communicated, indirectly and in plain sight, and to fictionalise that process even as a daydream would be to fictionalise the character of a person, which isn't so bad, after all, but I've never been able to do it)—and the long, detailed letters he wrote to my mother during the year he spent in Australia, working on a farm, for what reason I've no idea, but it must have been important enough for him to leave my mother behind even though he was in love with her, or certainly serious enough about her to propose to her before he left, in order (so my mother's telling goes) to ensure that she would wait for him while he was away, a proposal my mother declined (this offered to me as a lesson in self-worth, which I've never been able to distinguish fully from vanity), the open parenthesis intolerable to her without the guarantee that it would be resolved, and, perhaps above all, the marginalia which he left in a number of books which remained on the bookcase in the room we called the 'study' (the room in which I wrote that essay on Egypt I mentioned earlier, on a hot day in July, not feeling bad about copying and pasting large chunks of text into a word doc because, I remember thinking, lazily but not uninventively, that I couldn't really see the difference between using a single word that already existed and a whole paragraph of them, and, anyway, wasn't it the case that my reproduction of these words in a different context in itself constituted a fresh and original utterance, a view which later in life I would find to be in agreement with a number of tedious and manipulative writers but also with the Scottish poet G, a biography of whom I am supposed to be writing at this very moment and which I am neglecting in favour of writing this to you, A, who wrote that you cannot twice bring the same word into sound, a program I still subscribe to in theory, but which in practice—in the practice of life, that is, rather than art—serves as proof of the distance between the principles by which I read and those by which I live, since I can take pleasure in repetition in a work of art or a novel or poem, be open to and even celebrate the process of differentiation which repetition makes visible, but when my mother asks me for the seventh time (I count) during the same phone call, standing on the Meadows, in the freezing air, why we called our son K (she wants the reason to be that he is named after her favourite uncle, who I met once as a child, the night before my grandmother's funeral, which I was going to describe but, having had a couple of goes at it, realise it isn't relevant—even in its irrelevance—which makes me alert to the fact that even though the various clauses I've written up to this point have been put down 'at random', having 'followed the brush', as I puts it, connected only by their occurrence at moments when I found myself thinking of and wanting to write to you, who I can address precisely and only because I have invented your presence, I do on some level intuit some relation between them, some kind of formal pattern, though what that is I'm not yet sure) I experience that repetition as obtuse, a violation of the principle of attentiveness and variety in conversation which I didn't realise I held as a principle until it was violated, which leads me to ask myself strange or obvious questions, such as *why can't I experience my mother's conversation like a work of art*), including books on trees and plants and wildlife and Catholicism and also, more surprisingly, books of poetry, and even more surprisingly, books of *criticism* about poetry, including *Poets of the World*, and L's book about M and N (this enthusiasm for 'culture'—he also had a large collection of classical music records, which by the time I felt the impulse to listen to them as a teenager were too scratched to be played, though I remember testing out O's *Four Seasons*, and only slowly coming to the realisation that the glitches in the music were in fact unintentional, products of wear and deterioration, the material inscriptions of my father's listening, rather than deliberate striations in the work—was one of the reasons my father was suspected, by many of his teammates on the rugby team he captained and others in the town that was small enough for such rumours to be considered seriously damaging, to be gay, rumours which may or may not have contributed to the priest who had supervised my father's conversion refusing to allow his body to be buried in consecrated ground, the cause of his death being unclear, him being fit and healthy and up until the age of thirty unattached to any woman, and this taking place in 1989) but it's his edition of P, borrowed from and never returned to the library at the local Grammar School for Boys, that seems to me to offer the richest fragments from which this imagined person might be assembled, the unintelligible notes written in pencil in the margins of 'Birches' in particular, written when he was fourteen or fifteen, already a third of the way through his life (though the final tally was not yet counted) offer the co-ordinates of a space in which to imagine the teenage boy my father was still reading, somewhere in the seams of that poem, in that edition, which I carried round with me pretty much constantly for a few years, I remember in particular one day during the winter tuition fees were tripled, placing my hand on it inside my coat pocket, on my way to a protest (after skipping a shift at the market research company I was working at to pay for my MA—the project we were working on at the time was for the car insurance company AA, who had commissioned the market research company I worked for to conduct phone interviews with a random sample of the population in order to determine the ways in which their products and services could be altered in order to ensure future customer satisfaction, interviews which lasted usually around an hour, and for which time the interviewee received no compensation, but strange as it sounds we (by which I mean, me and the thirty or forty other call centre workers) had very little difficulty persuading large numbers of these total strangers —1000 over the course of three months, if I remember rightly—to participate in this unremunerated and tedious process, in which I would ask a long series of questions based on hypothetical scenarios, such as 'how would you feel if your car insurance premiums were tied to gender, can you please answer on a scale of 1 to 5 where 1 would be very unhappy and 5 would be very happy', and I think there was such a willingness on the part of the respondents to participate for a number of reasons, of course some of them may simply have been interested in car insurance, most or all may have had nothing better to do, but also, this is my guess, I suspect there was for many people something inviting about the prospect of being invited to speak about car insurance in purely numerical terms for an hour or so, something appealing about the guaranteed boredom of that activity, I could tell that some participants had after several minutes of questioning entered an almost meditative state, in which, upon being asked a question, they could respond on the scale of 1 to 5 with an almost eerie alacrity, as if the virtually transparent medium of 1–5 had granted them a degree of access to their desires and their gradations which everyday language, in its complexity and variety, was not only unable to achieve but actively inhibited, a speculation I allowed myself since even I as the interviewer experienced during this process a pleasurable simplification in the terms of engagement with the world, in which all choices were reduced to a narrow spectrum of personal preference, very happy to very unhappy, there was something childlike about it (and also about the exactness and confidence and fluency with which, after the first twenty minutes or so of questions, some respondents would deliver their numerical verdicts on possible future amendments to insurance policies or their implementation) but, at the same time, something complex in the delivery too, there was often something unexpectedly expressive in the hesitation over the boundary between 3 and 4 in particular, a hesitation which would become more frequent towards the end of the interview, in which I sensed that the respondents (and to some degree myself) were becoming aware of, and perhaps a little anxious about, their impending necessary return to the arena of non-numerical language, to words and sentences, to a situation in which preferences are often required to be supplemented with explanations or conditions or other, sometimes painfully elaborate contextual material, to considerations beyond those which the extremely focused internality the interview had obliged them to develop had brought to light, then there's the fact that the subject-matter was virtually impersonal or of a personal order so seemingly unexpressive that it was relinquished without resistance, which perhaps may not be possible any more, only ten years later, in which the expression of personal preference in a public sphere (over the phone, on social media) has been revealed to be a gesture potentially subject to, among other things, political manipulation, even the most innocuous question, asked in the simplest terms, even in numerical terms, about the content of our character or the way in which we view the behaviour of other people or the developments in a larger sense of the exterior world can be analysed in the context of hundreds of thousands of other responses in order to create the picture of a general trend, a pattern or movement of opinion, an index of feeling, an alarming thought, to feel that our own feelings, which feel so particular to us (they are inside us, they are closer to us than we are to ourselves, yet also somehow separate) are in fact driven by larger forces outside of ourselves, that we are in fact being *felt through*) with my friend Q, as we joined the group of perhaps a couple of hundred students and schoolchildren on the road outside the university's central administrative building, who, after a period of chanting and shouting and banner waving, moved slowly but purposefully downhill past the grammar school Q and I had both attended, and of which I now felt obscurely embarrassed (I always had a concise account of my scholarship ready, should anyone ask), down Park Street (I've only ever been punched once in my life, when I was fifteen, leaning against a restaurant window on this street, and even though it took place ten years before I was walking past that place as part of a large crowd, when I think of that incident it's as if I'm experiencing it at this very moment, or, rather, I'm always *about to experience it*—the punch is always about to land—so that it feels like what I am remembering is not so much the punch itself as my body's anticipation of it, the violent flinch in advance of the impact, a sensation which when I think of it feels, odd as it sounds, like it's actually happening again in my body, and so vivid is this sensation that it feels categorically inaccurate to think of it as a memory, unless, that is, we think of memory as actually not really occupying a position in the closed-off past, but as having the potential to irrupt into the present with all the force (even more, perhaps) of those incidents that occur in the present—though, in terms of our apprehension of reality, we literally live in the past, as an article I read the other day on Buzzfeed reminded me ('Just A Reminder That We're All Living in the Past'), but that refers to a past that's so recent as to seem not really past at all—I can feel it even now as I summon up the image of the man (boy, really) crossing the dark street, strangely exact in his trajectory—his body was following a line which terminated in my body —then as he entered the area I loosely thought of as my 'personal space', which never really makes itself fully visible until it is breached, his torso turning to the right then springing back in a forward motion so that his full bodily weight is propelled through the instrument of his arm, terminating in a clenched fist, and transferring itself into my left cheekbone), and all this time songs were being sung by the protestors, though I felt too embarrassed to join in, uncertain whether the embarrassment was down to the fact that I was walking next to Q, and we had never sung together or in front of each other before, or because I was insufficiently convinced of the sentiments or ideas the songs advanced ('No ifs, no buts, / No education cuts', for example, left me with a pathetic flicker of anxiety about the resistance to dialogue it implied (an experience of uncertainty or bewilderment I had again this weekend, during a protest on the Meadows against R's visit to Scotland, which we didn't make it to, H spent most of the day making her sign for the protest (which read 'the only baby who should be in a cage is you', with an accompanying picture), while I spent it trimming the hedge, though at the last minute H also ended up baking some gingerbread Ss, which K and I ended up selling in the street to passersby on the way to the protest, they were funny-looking gingerbreadmen, with accurate comb-overs and bright blue nappies, and I was pleased and proud to be sat in the street with my son, on the little chairs and table set which he normally uses for drawing, and on which we had laid out a plate of gingerbread Ts and a tupperware container for donations (which we had decided, after some quick googling, would be given to an organisation called the Immigrant Defence Fund), he was being very cute and was entertaining everyone, or most people, who walked past, by waving to them and asking if they wanted a biscuit, delightful stuff, though another part of me was—and I'm even a bit ashamed to admit it—a bit ashamed to be sitting on the pavement with a child rather than joining the protest proper, since it seemed like a maybe too on-the-nose illustration of the way in which the decision to have a family of one's own, to become a parent, entails a slight withdrawal from the larger social world, a focus on the immediate and the blood-relational, a voluntary self-marginalisation which much of the time actually feels involuntary, which represents a choice for a smaller collective pronoun than is possible—the *we* of the family, rather than the *we* of the social totality, if that was ever truly available—but, at the same time, another part of me was accepting of this opting out, even a little relieved by its necessity, by the feeling of immobilisation, the dramatic loss of agency, which having a child brings about—which extends from the practicalities of everyday life (you can't go out whenever you want, or do whatever you want) to the most intimate areas of interior life, by which I mean, as I have written either earlier or later, that when I had a child I registered perhaps for the first time what U calls the 'biology of feeling', which I experienced holding my son for the first time, overtaken by a feeling the only term for which I had available was happiness (I remember thinking the word slowly to myself, happiness, spelling it out, as though the duration of the word were somehow connected to the duration of the feeling), and I remember sobbing as I held him, my body throbbing with a feeling that he generated, and yet, and most of us will have experienced this, when we are overwhelmed or overtaken by feeling, there is the weird elation that comes with the feeling of access to an experience that transcends the personal, we are entering or entered by a state which, even if experienced in isolation, is collective in texture, the particulars of our own sensibilities are so swept away by the hormonal surge which drives the feeling that we become indistinct, and a line is drawn from us vertically through time, into the past and future, and part of what is moving or affecting is that we understand that what we are feeling in that moment is identical to or similar to what our own parents felt when they first held us, and their own parents before them (though, of course, this idea of vertical connection to earlier moments in time through feeling is a kind of delusion, since I've no idea how my father or his father or however many great-grandfathers before would have felt at that moment, I don't know if they would have felt happy or would have been culturally prepared for that surge of endorphins in the way my body was, or even if they had experienced that surge would have had the language to describe or even conceive of it as an expression of happiness, and I've no idea how feelings will be experienced or described or rendered in the future), an anonymising sense of connection which also makes me wary, in the sense that I'm wary of protests, of the affecting tones of collective singing, of the movements of large crowds in unison, which was why I felt kind of relieved to be sat on the pavement with my son rather than joining the protest against V, about whom I suspected I didn't feel the same level of anger as other people (H included, she seems actually wounded by the things he has done, and it is her capacity for feeling for others, her essential porousness, that I admire, since I have so little of that capacity myself), I mainly experience a sense of irritation that this is the future we are having to live in, which feels very much like a bad universe parallel to the 'main channel' of time (or a paraphrase so inaccurate that key details of the plot have been completely disfigured) one in which even the most implausible scenarios have to be played out, in real time and in the most minute detail, to uphold infinity's reputation for exhaustiveness, and this feeling of irritation isn't quite mobilising enough for me to want to get up and do anything about it, since though it usually begins with or is activated by W or X as its original prompt, it soon dissolves into a generalised mood of irritation that is so extensive and all-encompassing that it becomes both attachable to, and receivable from, any object or person in the vicinity), past the council offices on College Green, left round a sharp corner then after several hundred metres into the shopping district called Broadmead, into the recently-built development called Cabot Circus—named after the Venetian explorer Y, a Venetian navigator and explorer whose 1497 discovery of the coast of North America under the commission of Z of England was the first European exploration of the mainland of North America since the Norse visits to Vinland in the eleventh century, a man connected to Bristol because it was from that city, in the late 15th century the second-largest seaport in England, that voyages in search of Hy-Brazil (a phantom island said to lie in the Atlantic Ocean west of Ireland, described in Irish myths as being cloaked in mist except one day every seven years, and whose name—the etymology of which is unknown, but in Irish tradition is thought to come from the Irish Uí Breasail (meaning 'descendants (i.e., clan) of Bresail'), one of the ancient clans of northeastern Ireland—has no connection to the name of the country of Brazil, despite the similarity)had been launched regularly since 1480, and from whence S (or U) set sail in the winter of 1497—which had since its opening rendered large areas of tattered, 1990s developments (including The Galleries, a shopping centre a couple of hundred metres away, which I remember once being as gleamingly inviting as Cabot Circus then appeared, but now has more unoccupied than occupied units) redundant, and in this commercial space the singing of the protestors took on a new note of joyful defiance, as though the shopping centre itself were somehow implicated in the decision to commercialise higher education, an intuition which

I felt without evidence or understanding to be basically correct, at which point I began to sing (an odd thing, incidentally, has started to happen as I type this passage, which is that because I am inserting this parenthetical sentence into the body of an already-large body of text, I am typing at a speed the word processor is unable to keep up with, not because I am a fast typer (I am not) but because every word I am typing necessitates a spatial adjustment of the entire textual body (or at least the text beneath this passage), a consequence of which is that when I have finished typing my sentence or sentence-fragments and I look up at the screen—I am not a touch typer, I have to look at the letters on the keyboard and hope that they are being accurately rendered as words—I can see the sentence or sentence-fragments appearing to be slowly, letter-by-letter, typed out in front of me, as though by a fractionally-delayed iteration of myself), and though I don't remember exactly what I sang, whatever it was that I sang seemed to go on for in an inordinately long time (something happens to time during a protest that I can't quite work out, I don't know what it is or how it happens, but it feels like time stretches out, becomes a little thicker and more material as the seconds and the minutes and hours pass, perhaps, as B suggests, it's just that for much of the time during a protest nothing happens, there is often no *event*, once the songs have stopped and the conflicts with the antagonist (whether the police or some other force) have resolved temporarily into a truce or suspension of immediate hostilities, and the practical business of staying warm and using the space you have secured has come into play, time seems to slow down, and it becomes boring, though I say this based on experiences largely prior to the era of the smartphone (perhaps this experience is itself dated, and time is more portable than it used to be, or we now have our own temporalities or timelines governed by what we are looking at, rather than where we are, I don't know), back in 2011, when H and I spent a day at the UCL occupation, H with her camera (which, from the moment we entered the occupied room, I was envious of, as the the camera allowed her to float around the room, almost invisible, almost concealed and enclosed within the sphere of a discrete, deferred time, placing her lens close to or far away from people's faces, overhearing conversations, adjusting the settings with fine hand movements, but it also allowed her to just stand still with no expression on her face and with no burden of responsibility to become involved, to be engaged, because she was only partly there as herself, she was also a medium through which the later experience of the present moment was being enabled, and as such wasn't to be disturbed, whereas I had no excuse for my non-participation, my peculiar stasis, sat silently in the back row of a bank of chairs), and though the day was divided into periods for discussion, then a (terrible) poetry reading, given by three radical poets (one literally dressed as C) who afterwards stood looking moody having their photos taken by a young student with his analogue Leica, then a lecture given by a hugely bearded and corduroyed man from SOAS about how time dilates during occupations, something about them operating as bubbles suspended within the system of productive labour time, but also, maybe more interestingly, that because of this temporal distortion the occupation can be considered a negative image of a diametrically opposed social space, the casino, which is a notoriously clockless zone, a site of expensive leisure which can be approached as a socially sanctioned means for the destruction of excessive labour time and financial capital, as the quotation of D from E's work indicates, and which in its seemingly endless deferral of narrative events (or, rather, its suspension of narrative closure, until, that is, a bank account has run dry, and a patron ruined) also stretches time into a fluid, frictionless and banal medium, which is only reactivated at the point when the person emerges from the casino into the blinding light of the suddenly advancing day), for as long as it took the lengthy column of protestors (which was much more biological-looking-and-feeling than 'column' suggests, a churning, rippling, distending thing) to pivot and make its way back up the hill towards the central administrative building, where it finally stalled or pooled or congealed, in the freezing afternoon, and where within minutes the police on foot and on horseback began to form their kettle around us, so that what began as a dispersed and shapeless conglomeration of bodies soon appeared—to my eyes, as I stood on a grassy bank overlooking this scene, after I had ducked out of the forming kettle, because I had been too afraid to stay in the group, and had retreated outside the ring of police, ashamed and embarrassed and relieved to have opted out, to have escaped, to have put my own safety above that of others or above the thing we were protesting against—as a shape as exactly rounded as a cataract, with the breath of the protestors increasingly visible above them as a hovering cloud, opaque and amorphous, an image I shouldn't really have been able to record, since I later told many people that I *had* been trapped in the kettle, that I'd waited the afternoon out in the freezing air, which didn't feel just like a 'lie' in the conventional sense, but also somehow felt like a kind of 'theft' from those protestors who had been committed enough to stay in the kettle while Q and I had escaped it, and from my elevated vantage was able to observe the goings-on from a position of relative safety, and when the afternoon wore on I was able to retreat to Q's house, which was warm and comfortable, and we could congratulate each other in an excited and confused and guilty way on our involvement in political action which, as we now know, had no effect on government policy, it's perhaps the worst lie or theft I've ever committed, and one I've told repeatedly, though one I didn't call to mind the other night, as I was having dinner with some people after a poetry reading I'd participated in at a university, and because we were struggling to sustain a conversation with one another, and I was already a little drunk, I asked the one from the group I thought I liked the most, a historian who had only a few seconds before mentioned something about stealing, what the worst theft she'd ever committed was, which, after an expression of surprise, followed by a few seconds of thought, during which time her face became taut, inward-turned and unintelligible, she revealed to have been an artificial nail from the salon her mother used to visit and to which she had been taken on one occasion, aged nine or ten, a nail which had been displayed on a disembodied white mannequin hand and decorated in such a lavish and inviting manner (painted a bright pink and crusted with tiny fake jewels) that she had taken it home to treasure and to handle and to study and to imagine onto the ends of her own fingers, and which her mother had somehow discovered (whether she had confessed or if the stolen nail had been discovered by chance we weren't told—or perhaps we were and I can't remember), resulting in her mother dragging her back to the salon to return the nail and apologise to the nail artist, who, when the child historian apologised to her, smiled and said it was alright, there being an implication in the telling of this detail that the nail artist had been more pleased that a child would consider a material of her work beautiful enough to steal than annoyed that it had been stolen in the first place, after which disclosure (which had relaxed us all, the slightly desperate and risky solicitation of a personal anecdote had come off, and we, three slightly drunk men, appeared or actually were impressed by the eloquence of the historian and touched and invigorated by the sophistication of the story, which seemed subtly sceptical about guilt and judgement, and were readying ourselves for our own disclosures, nervously and excitedly, though we were all conscious of the need to suppress this feeling of excitement about the opportunity to tell, of the necessity of performing an equilibrium of desire and control, so I turned to the man sitting next to me, a Virginian playwright whom I'd offended minutes before by asking from which part of Ireland he hailed (we were in a loud, wood-panelled room, with perhaps a hundred people lined on both sides of five banks of long tables, and in this hard, somehow flat-seeming environment our voices took on the quality of a kind of collective bark, plateauing just above the level of comfort and just below the level of discomfort, a horribly boxed-in-seeming noise, like the noise of claustrophobia itself, if it has a noise, as I'm recalling it now I'm reminded of a question that had once been posed in a physics class at school —*can you trap light in a box*—which I've just googled and the answer to which is an emphatic *no*) and asked him the same question, *what's the worst thing you've ever stolen*, and he smiled with what looked like pleasure and said something like *so as an undergraduate I was very unhappy, I had come from rural*

Virginia, lived on a farm just outside a small town, not been exposed to much culture, or other types of people, a pretty insular upbringing you know, and though I should say I love my family very much, I had a very happy childhood, or at least thought it was a happy childhood as I was living it, it was only afterwards, when I'd grown up a bit and gone out into the world, I had the benefit of hindsight to understand really how limited my conception of happiness was at the time, as a child, you know, it was the classic playing outside all day, feeding and tending to the animals kind of stuff, but when I got into the outside world I realised that there was a much more complex or at least varied happiness available, there were different components to experience and what I came to think of as happiness was in fact a description of the balance between these different aspects or components of a whole life, anyway, I had been a happy child, or had thought of myself as such, and then I got to college and was suddenly confronted with the knowledge of the limitation of my conception of happiness up to that point, there were all these people who were so different from me, who came from different worlds, who had their own versions of what it meant to be happy which were so different from mine, and which, at the time, seemed much better versions, they seemed to be about your relationship with culture and society and politics and other places and family and sex, and the intensity and variety of these other people's lives just kind of appalled me, and as a result I just shrunk back into myself, I started not going out, just staying in my room, drinking and reading F, trying somehow to convert this feeling of panic and reticence that had come upon me into something productive, I guess, which was when I started writing plays, you know, or at least began to transcribe conversations between imagined speakers, as a way of socialising without having to actually see or speak to anyone, I still kind of prefer it to actually talking to other people, no offence, ha ha, but anyway this period of withdrawal lasted for most of my first semester, and for much of that time the only occasion I'd leave my room except to eat would be to go to a class run by this professor, G, who was a novelist who taught a kind of introduction to writing class, you did a bit of poetry and a bit of fiction and a bit of drama, and I remember because I was very unhappy for that semester, I was feeling very depressed and appalled by the smallness of my life and the limited conception of happiness I had operated under as a child, all basically class-related stuff, I wrote this piece for G's seminar in which, maybe unsurprisingly, two characters discuss the merits of suicide, in what I intended to be a kind of anxious and comic and vaguely European way, but which, when it was read out in class by two of my classmates, did not seem funny in the slightest, both of these classmates seemed very reluctant to read it, and appeared kind of horrified by what they were having to say out loud, they kept looking up at one another as if they were trying to decide whether to stop or whether to go on, and it seemed to me like the only reason they managed to make it to the end of the scene was because they hadn't resolved this sub-dialogue about continuation which was going on between them, in the form of meaningful looks and facial expressions, as they were reading my symposium on suicide, but anyway they did make it to the end of the scene, after which a kind of deathly silence hung in the room, and I remember thinking during that silence that maybe I had written the scene with the intention of taking its reception in class as the deciding factor, that is, if it went well I'd cheer up, but if it bombed then I'd kill myself, it wasn't a premeditated position but I realised it very clearly as it was happening, this terrible silence which was present in the room almost as a physical entity, like, oh, this was why you were writing that, to see what you're going to do, like a straw poll on your existence, OK, pretty dramatic I know, anyway this silence went on for a long time before G cleared his throat and said, well that wasn't exactly a musical, which generated some nervous laughter and made me feel like he was ridiculing me, or maybe just trying to relax the room, or something, but then he went on to give this measured and incisive critique of the piece, which was really a great deal more eloquent and purposeful and structured than the piece itself was, and I remember feeling really boosted by it at the time, but also vaguely sceptical too, in the sense that I guess I was a little afraid that my piece—which had meant a lot to me, you know, it turned out that I'd been hanging my life on its success—was becoming just a kind of handy occasion for G to espouse some pre-existing opinions about dramatic structure or the problematic nature of dialogue, but even with that doubt lingering it was clear that he'd perceived enough about the piece and the person writing it to know that his response was going to be important, which was why he wasn't wholly positive about it, I think, he criticised it in places, carefully and strategically, with the intention I think of leaving me something to do, something to correct, giving me an activity the completion of which would require at least another week of existence, which perhaps sounds like an overreading of a small gesture, but which I can assure you is not, since I came to know G pretty well after that class, I started to go to see him a couple of times a week in his office, often for a couple of hours at a time, we would just sit there talking about anything, and he never made me feel like I had to leave or that I was encroaching on his time, quite the opposite, in fact, often when I knocked on his door and came in he'd shout, ah, relief at last, though I know he was a busy man and also struggling with his own writing, I don't know, maybe it was a relief for him to talk to a morose undergraduate every now and then, so even in the next semester, and through the next couple of years, a long time after I'd stopped taking his class and any pretext for our meeting had evaporated, I would go and see him, without our ever having discussed the nature of my visits, and I grew to truly depend upon these visits, which, now, after years of psychoanalysis, I realise were roughly psychoanalytic in structure, in a number of ways but most importantly in the fact that he would encourage me to tell the same stories over and over again, something which at first I was a little bemused by, you know, and I would make a joke about him having fallen asleep again, which was maybe not that far off the mark, sometimes I thought that this request for me to repeat was a coping mechanism for him to try and make these long visits from me bearable, you know, him asking me to keep talking so that he could conclude the daydream he'd been having while I told the story for the first time, but he would do this with increasing frequency as the years passed, so that by the time I was in my final year these visits would take the form of me rocking up, talking about anything that had come up since we last met, and him asking me to repeat certain stories wholesale or certain small episodes from within larger stories, or asking for repeat versions of stories I'd told days, weeks or even months earlier, without offering any justification for the request, and, sure, at times I wondered if it was an exertion of power of some kind, or a way of giving himself some kind of pleasure, asking me to speak in this way, directing my conversation, and this may well have been the case, but there was also an element which was certainly instructional, and beneficial for me, in the sense that, without his having said anything, by the time I'd retold a story for the third time I could see it mapped out in front of me almost as a diagram, I could see the ways the narrative branched off at certain points, and how those different branches represented different kinds of moral or ideological inflection, or something, I became extremely self-conscious about the whole experience of speaking in his presence, actually, though with the caveat that I also felt an extreme sense of freedom with my speech, knowing that anything I said was likely to be subject to an indefinite number of later revisions, there was this extreme sense of provisionality to those hours I spent talking to him that felt somehow like training for something, writing, maybe, or just living, I'm not sure, but I had reached a point where I had so internalised the imagined audience of G that I found myself addressing my thoughts towards him throughout my day, my whole waking life occurred as if adjacent to him, and of course there were times when I found myself wondering if I was in love with him, though I was straight, or thought I was, this hadn't really been tested against experience, but, you know, I'd never been in love, so thought maybe this was what it was like, and it was during the period where I was trying to classify this feeling of his constant presence alongside or within me that he killed himself, entirely unexpectedly, it was a complete shock for me and, according to anyone I spoke to, for everyone else as well, though after he died some details came out about his life, including, maybe most importantly, that he'd split up from his wife several years before, without having told anyone and without anyone apparently noticing, a wife that he was totally estranged from, even though she'd been the closest thing to family he had in his life, which was the saddest and most shocking though perhaps not surprising thing, the fact that aside from his ex-wife, who wanted nothing to do with him or his estate after he died, there was nobody to deal with his possessions, his papers, and all that stuff, and there was a lot of it, there were dozens of bookcases and four or five filing cabinets in his office absolutely rammed with drafts and letters and heavily annotated editions of I and L and whoever else, so by some circuitous process it became known to the department that G and I had been close, probably one of the closest things to a friend he had had in recent years, and since by that point I'd started a literature PhD there it was decided that I should be entrusted with the responsibility of sorting through his files and create some kind of provisional guide to them so that the university library could decide whether or not they should go to the trouble of cataloguing and making available his archive, during which process, as I was sorting through various folders, which were organised—well, that's probably the wrong word—which were just stuffed full of random materials from throughout his life, so I just ended up tipping them out on the floor, one by one, in the hope that I could separate them into piles and into a comprehensible system, and it was during this process, tipping out folder after folder of the life's work of a dear friend, that I discovered a small number of polaroids, of a young, of a very young boy, a child, absolutely, and in some of these photographs he was clothed and in others not, but he was doing nothing in particular, just sat on a bed or on the floor, not doing anything pornographic or even vaguely provocative, just sitting there, sometimes smiling or sometimes expressionless, but never, I don't think, frightened-looking, though I suppose it's difficult to tell if someone is really frightened just from the expression on their face, and I remember sitting in his room, the room I had spent so many hours in over the previous few years, and wondering what these photos meant, who this boy was or had been, and who my friend was, and what this discovery meant, and I confess I also thought of his work, and what it had meant to me, and to others I knew, and without thinking it through in any detail—and as I was not thinking it through I knew exactly what I was doing, I knew very exactly that I knew I was considering the issue properly—I decided to burn the photos then and there, in the trash can of his very own office, and I never told anyone about it, after which we didn't really know what to say (and in the silence that followed I found myself wondering why the playwright had told us this story, what effect he was intending to create, what he got out of it, and if he had told it before—something about the structure of its telling suggested this was not the first time—partly because I know from experience that once we disclose something to someone, anyone, once we admit that something exists (or we claim it exists), whether it's a *secret* or just a fact about ourselves we haven't disclosed yet, for innocent or innocuous or serious reasons, then because of the pleasure the act can involve—the pleasure of release or transmission, of having opened a vent, which, I tells us, in some ways represents a wilful breaking or disabling of the self, a ruining of its prior form, a gesture which in part is intended to solicit an act of repair on the part of the addressee to whom the secret is revealed, and which tells us something straightforward, perhaps, about the dynamic between the person who discloses a secret and the person who agrees to or is obliged to hear it (due to my upbringing the formal structure of the priest and confessant springs to mind, one which is replicated by the relationship between parent and child, at least in part, since what is being asked for by both the confessing sinner and the child revealing a secret to the parent is the love forgiveness expresses, the disclosure of the secret is a kind of a brokenness which is solved by the loving one rebuilding us partly in their own image, M suggests, though the dynamic becomes more complicated and the formal relation of priest and confessant becomes less important when we are in a relationship with another person, in which the roles of confessant and pardoner circulate more freely, or at least should do if the structure of the relationship isn't going to become mistakable for the structure of priest and confessant or parent and child, which, if that happens, can be the moment at which a notion of unhappiness or dissatisfaction in a relationship can crystallise, that is, when one partner realises that this circulation of roles, this system of mutual dependency, of self-breaking and mutual rebuilding, has stalled, and that the terms of engagement with one another have settled stably into a format which is recognisable as something else, *I already have two children*, H will sometimes say to me, when I have forgotten something important or left a mess around the house, *I can't look after you as well*, a statement which usually, when I'm thinking about such things (a small crisis in our relationship usually leads me to instruct myself to think, *think about this*, I will say, or, rather, think to myself, which as I'm doing it does make me wonder what I am normally doing, it's not like I'm not thinking, I guess just behaving in an intuitive or habituated way, which normally works well enough, my existing memories and understanding of how to behave to make our life enjoyable, seem normally sufficient on a day-to-day basis, but they become suddenly inadequate in moments like this when H tells me she is tired of there being a significant overlap in how she sees me and how she sees our children, and so I have to start thinking, start being deliberate and self-reflective, and there is a tension in this moment, a feeling of resistance to this self-consciousness, since, according to N, one of the ways in which happiness in a relationship is experienced is through the feeling of 'being oneself' or 'feeling real' with the other person, a state of naturalness and of oneness with which this impulse to *think* conflicts, its introduction seems a form of artifice in what should be a wholly naturalised process of everyday living, though, of course, despite it being one of the most common experiences in life, there is very little that can be naturalised about the experiencing of living life with small children, since every day is, in a sense, a minor, ordinary crisis, a crisis which, in the ongoing moment of it, feels historical in its dimensions though the terms in which it is conducted are entirely ordinary (that feels quite vague, so for example one of the historical-feeling things about the experience of the present moment as it's shaped by children is its radical contraction in scope, when on a Tuesday people ask me *how was your weekend*, I often literally can't recall anything about that period of time, which feels displaced to a distance far beyond its actual distance in time, a new relation to the past brought about by our children that is replicated in a dramatic foreshortening in our conception of the future, for example, before we had children our notion of the present extended weeks, even months in advance (it was in fact something H and I would occasionally worry about, whether we were too invested in our plans for the future to pay enough attention to the present) but now we have days where the notion of 'tomorrow' seems unmanageably, exhaustingly complex) if only in the sense that because children change so rapidly—B started to walk last week, prompting a substantial recalibration of household objects—we are obliged to think about our environment and how we behave in a way that we otherwise wouldn't, and this demand to think, to constantly be alert to change, is central to my understanding of what is difficult about the experience of parenting, the difficulty of it being the experience of our children's resistance to our efforts to naturalise the process of everyday experience, something which, perhaps unsurprisingly, is what makes their presence as people in the room—as I write they are drawing monsters at their activity table—so heavily felt) causes me to start behaving in a 'parental' way towards her, I make her a tea and a hot water bottle, I try to make her comfortable, and she relaxes into the role of being cared for, of being a child, she even starts to speak in a childish way, sometimes, as if the register of childishness or cuteness itself, so removed from the register of orderly, purposeful and self-conscious thinking in which she conducts most of her life, is itself a form of physical comfort or relief), since it is an obligation, of course, and one undertaken usually on faith, since if somebody asks us *can you keep a secret* (has there been anybody in human history who has, when asked that delicious and alarming question, simply said *no, I don't want it, keep it to yourself, I'm not bothered*) we are agreeing very much in the abstract, we don't know anything specific about what is about to be revealed and so we are exposing ourselves, making ourselves vulnerable to learning something we may immediately or eventually decide we would rather not have known, a possibility which makes the act of agreeing to hear a secret seem almost as reckless, if not more so, than the act of disclosing one—there is an increased desire to repeat that disclosure, to keep telling, to repeat the pattern of exposure and observation, to stage the scene of being seen, or at least that's my experience of it, I enjoy revealing things about myself that surprise or draw the attention of others (perhaps even, or especially, this revelation of how much I like revealing myself), a self-indulgent and childlike pleasure, which is not necessarily to say a bad one, but it makes me wonder sometimes about some of the things I do, the cruel or wounding or spiteful things I sometimes say to people, it makes me wonder if what I'm really seeking, when I behave in an unforgivable fashion or say something unnecessarily close-to-the-bone or flagrantly unfair about a person I'm speaking to or a mutual friend or a writer I dislike, is simply *a stage on which to parade my disgrace*, a phrase I'm half-remembering from O's essay on P, 'Confessions (Excuses)' (in an earlier iteration, 'The Purloined Ribbon') which I teach every year, alongside his essays on literary history and the resistance to theory, but which I concentrate on in particular, since much of the class tends to revolve around a discussion on the nature of R's writing in light of his terrible behaviour in many spheres of life, from his polygamy to his financial misdealing to his anti-semitism and collaborationist activities in wartime Belgium, which often enlarges to a discussion of the relationship between people and texts, and how responsible one can be for the other, especially since, in one respect, this is what the S essay is about, and this separation is exactly what T argues for, in the sense that his proposition of the essential *autonomy of the text*—is that his proposition, I can hardly remember, but irrespective of whether that's actually the case, for me that argument for the autonomy of the text is now located, no, stored, in this essay—has the effect of diminishing or completely erasing the impact his own personal guilt can have on the work he produced, something I found myself thinking about in the pause that followed the playwright's story, since the question of what to do with the huge volume of art produced by disgraced men—a broader context his story had, perhaps knowingly, engaged—had around that time become central in the culture for what seemed the first time in my life (the question of, say, what to do with the films of U or V, which I started watching in my teens, seemed at the time to be largely treated with unflustered uncertainty) and the answers to it seemed so numerous and unsatisfactory, and I felt the insufficiency of my thoughts about them routinely, I had, for example, set for a recent class a piece of video art by W, only in the intervening time between the syllabus being put together and the class itself it had been revealed that over the past few years he has systematically groomed underage girls for sex, a fact which has a particularly disturbing effect on the work itself, since one of its trademark gestures is the use of misspelling, a *faux-naif* characteristic intended, I'd originally thought, to undercut the authority of the artist, to open the work up to audiences that might find the gesture hospitable or sociable, and to guarantee only a difficult assimilation into institutions of art production and reception (art schools, journals etc.) which valorised expertise or skill, and to point towards the potential for *pleasure* and new creation enabled by error and inability, or something, but which now appeared to me merely to be a tool in his grooming of adolescents, an expert kind of ventriloquism of a childish or adolescent register of speech employed to manipulate, and which was eerily absent from the apology he posted on Twitter a few days ago, in which he concluded by saying something like *ultimately I think it's right that I've been exposed*, but I showed the video anyway, since I'd thought it worth showing only a few days earlier, if only to use it as a case study in acclimatising to a shift in receptive context precipitated by the release of new knowledge (I find myself saying embarrassing things like this in class, and then immediately regretting them—sometimes I feel like I regret so many of the things I say that the regret has actually started to precede the saying, so that I find myself lodged in what feels like a permanent state of pre-regret, which has the effect of endowing silence, or deciding not to speak, with an almost luxurious quality), to perform for the students (and ask them to perform for or with me) this graduated shift in understanding, *since I don't think*, I ended up saying to the class, *that the act of erasing this person—from the syllabus, from memory, from the screen, in the way X was removed at the editing stage from the film* All the Money in the World *(a 2017 crime thriller film directed by Y and written by Z) is necessarily the best approach, though now I think about it I have taken off my syllabus over the past two years an essay about rhyme by a poet who turned out to be a paedophile and a novel about drugs written by a rapist and a short story by a serial abuser of women, who pre-empted his own exposure with a piece of non-fiction in which he implied that his own sexual abuse as a child had resulted in him mistreating partners throughout his adult life, which is probably the case, I guess, by which I mean the one is probably connected to the other, but, and here I struggle to formulate what I think I mean, I find it very difficult to engage either with these defences or with responses to these defences which dismiss them out of hand, since on the one hand there is a broad acknowledgement of the structural nature of the behaviour (that the culture of toxic masculinity is in itself partly culpable for these actions, that people model their own relationships on those of their own parents and family, which they can't help, and in many cases are severely damaged individuals who have experienced trauma which they are unable to manage), and on the other the understanding that they remain individuals who act more-or-less freely, who choose to behave in a harmful way towards others, and if you were to defend their actions on the basis of the chain of events, always receding infinitely into the past, which led up to the moment in which their actions took place, then everything and everyone could be excusable, so it's the question of where and how to blame one another which is causing me such confusion, and I find myself suspended in my permanent condition of doubt, unable to come to any meaningful or useful conclusion*, after which there was quite a long silence, before I said, *I don't know, what do you think*), and I quite wanted to get up and leave, or to ask a long series of detailed questions about the story, but for whatever reason I didn't, and after this prolonged silence, the character of which was hard to determine, I turned to the other poet who had read that night (in an exaggerated 'let's move on' way, which was at least half-serious), a man whose name I've forgotten for the moment, call him B, whom I had initially been really impressed by, since he was handsome and well-dressed and spoke in a measured fashion, and because earlier in the evening, before the lapse in conversation which led me to start up this whole *confess your theft* business, when I or someone else had made a remark, he had seemed more often than not to disagree with it in a very slight way, which is a risky thing to do with people you've only just met, but which rather than making him seem contrary or belligerent in fact seemed indicative of a confidence not just in himself but in everyone else and in all of our abilities to negotiate complexity, and, strangely and most impressively, this disagreement was also expressed in such a way that it seemed like he was somehow, through his disagreement, actually *agreeing* with whatever had been initially said, or, rather, the localised disagreement with the previous remark

signalled the presence of a larger agreement the
conversation was working towards, as a collective act
in which we were all engaged, the lineaments of which
were yet to be defined, so I was pretty impressed,
I liked him and I wanted to impress him too, I think,
especially when it turned out that he was older than I
was, and had two children slightly older than my own,
I began to ask him about what I should expect from
slightly older toddlers, if he had any advice, how his
relationship was coping after the arrival of children,
the distribution of labour at home (which in
recent months, I explained, since H had gone back
to working every available hour on a new series of
photographs, had shifted radically, since I was now
solely responsible for every aspect of life at home, the
cooking, cleaning, bills, childcare, and so on, all of
which I performed as best I could while also 'working'
'full-time', though I was always conscious of only doing
everything by halves, any action half-consciously,
that is, while I was hoovering or tidying or playing
I felt I was only semi-there, I was always thinking
about some other thing, such as a piece of literary
criticism I was planning or a poem I was thinking
about writing or some pressing administrative task,
but also—and this was less clear to me—I felt that
recently my sense of presence in my own body had
become strangely displaced, in that while the children were playing or fighting in another room—they
are at this moment aged 4 and 2—I thought of myself
as present as much 'in my hearing' as in my hands

pushing the hoover about or cleaning the surfaces, which is to say the deictics of my body had become scattered, suspended or virtualised, a feeling which conditioned how I felt as I was writing, too—as I am writing this now, in fact, with the children working together on a Peppa Pig puzzle in the living room, which may partly explain why I have continued to write in this drifting, scrambled way, since the idea of writing things down in a linear fashion, one thing after another, would seem to require a reorganisation of experience and an effort of concentration of which I don't currently feel capable, even though as I read back through what I've written, following the brush of the days, link by link, it seems to make no sense in terms of sequence or cause and effect, and refuses to create or allow that feeling of absorption which I often want when I read, that total spherical effect of placement within time which I get when I read *Middlemarch*, which I opened at random this morning as though opening a door into an entirely different way of being, the rhythm of another life), that kind of thing, and as I was asking these questions I noticed myself imitating his mannerisms in a low-key way, for example, taking a little bit more time with my speech than I normally do, pausing to select the most accurate words or to perform that careful selection, in the hope that he would think of me, *oh this guy really thinks about what he's going to say before he says it*, which is what I was thinking about him when I asked him something and he took a few moments, without any apparent self-consciousness, to really consider what he thought or felt about it, during which process he would look away from me, and his eyes would be directed slightly above or to the side of my head, and would start to move in a rapid and barely-perceptible side-to-side motion, and though they seemed especially animated at this moment they also appeared visibly vacated—that is, the movements of his eyes, which obviously were still seeing in a biological sense, were being directed by a different kind of sight, one pointed inwards, towards what, exactly, I don't know—and after this strangely observable search of his interior (or the performance of this search) was completed, he would reply in the measured manner I've mentioned above, in complete sentences, with an often impressively (and sometimes eccentrically) complex syntax, which suggested that though what he was saying had been premeditated in some respects—as a kind of general intention to respond in a particular fashion, maybe—the actual form in which it was eventually articulated was something of an improvisation (as all speech is, I guess, or most), and naturally enough this was something I found myself copying as well, though almost as soon as I became aware that this was what was happening (the copying, that is) another part of me —the part that finds my desire to imitate weak and even repulsive—started to derail the imitation, to cut off sentences halfway through, leaving thoughts incomplete, I found myself using an unusual number of colloquialisms, saying *uh* and *like* and *I dunno*, sometimes even being wilfully obtuse, all in an attempt to differentiate myself from the subtleties of this man's conversation, though, of course, soon enough any embarrassment I had felt about the initial imitative gesture was overtaken by a more potent embarrassment about the obviousness and artificiality of my attempts at self-assertion, since the self I was asserting was little more than an improvised foil, a fictionalised antithesis to the person I was talking to, a realisation that left me trapped in a state of narrow equivocation between acquiescence and resistance, capitulation and assertion, fiction and fiction, wondering all the time if I would ever become a real person, so I experienced a few minutes of serious melancholy, but, unexpectedly, after this initial series of exchanges, as the evening went on and this poet had more and more wine, it gradually became apparent that he was becoming increasingly aware of his social success, and with this awareness came a slight alteration in his tone or manner, he began talking about himself in a bit too much detail when asked an only lightly inquisitive question, he began telling stories from his past to illustrate his points rather than making observations based on the discussion to hand, and it seemed to me that he had begun to lose the struggle that he had been winning so emphatically earlier in the evening, that is, the struggle not to find himself very interesting, a struggle in which he was ultimately and catastrophically defeated when,

after dinner was over and we were sat drinking
more wine at one end of the very long wooden table,
in the aftermath of the playwright's disturbing monologue, I asked him about his worst theft, in response
to which he initially paused for a long time (by this
point such pauses no longer gave the impression that
he was carefully weighing up his views or his expressive options, but self-indulgently taking pleasure in
listening to the silence of others who have, for better
or worse, committed to listening to what he was
about to say) before beginning to tell a scandalously
long story, which took perhaps twenty-five minutes
to tell, and was so ill-judged it was hard to know
how to react with my face, I realised this when, as he
was speaking, I found myself thinking about my face
(*c.* 1300, 'the human face, a face, facial appearance
or expression, likeness, image', from Old French face
'face, countenance, look, appearance' (12c.), from
Vulgar Latin *facia (source also of Italian faccia),
from Latin facies 'appearance, form, figure', and sec-
ondarily 'visage, countenance', which probably is
literally 'form imposed on something' and related
to facere 'to make' (from PIE root *dhe- 'to set, put'),
replaced Old English andwlita 'face, countenance'
(from root of wlitan 'to see, look')—recently, when
K wants me to look at something, and I'm distracted
and pretend to be paying attention but am in fact obviously doing something else, he gets very frustrated
(a frustration I remember very well feeling with my
mother when I was a child, at this layering of attention

which was detectable on her face), and says Daddy, look with your face—and ansyn, ansien, the usual word (from the root of seon 'see'), words for 'face' in Indo-European commonly are based on the notion of 'appearance, look', and are mostly derivatives from verbs for 'to see, look' (as with the Old English words, Greek prosopon, literally 'toward-look', Lithuanian veidas, from root *weid- 'to see', etc.), but in some cases, as here, the word for 'face' means 'form, shape', in French, the use of face for 'front of the head' was given up 17c. and replaced by visage (older vis), from Latin visus 'sight' from late 14c. as 'outward appearance (as contrasted to some other reality)', also from late 14c. as 'forward part or front of anything', also 'surface (of the earth or sea), extent (of a city)', typographical sense of 'part of the type which forms the letter' is from 1680s) and the shapes it makes and what they represent in a way I hardly ever do, most acutely at one point, towards the end of his epic anecdote, when he was describing in some detail his commandeering of a motorcycle in order to take his outrageously provocative manuscript to the government offices of the 'corrupt African state' in which the anecdote was taking place so that it could be scrutinised by a censor, and he began making rev-ing motions with his hands, I wanted very much at that moment for my face to express that I found him and his straightforward fantasy of colonialist adventure ludicrous, so I raised my eyebrows a fraction, but I also didn't feel sufficiently confident to be rude, since

I was drunk and feeling like an unreal person, and sometimes when I feel like that I misread situations, sometimes quite badly, so in this spirit of humility I lowered my eyebrows a fraction, and also because the historian—who was by this point sat next to me—was a woman of colour whom I had (perhaps wrongly) presumed to be gay, and because the anecdote seemed to be a kind of white saviour narrative in which this guy had written a play about homosexuality in order to educate or provoke homophobic Ugandans (not, obviously, that I thought there was anything wrong with the idea of provoking homophobes with literature, but) she seemed like the person who might find it most intimately objectionable, so I wanted to at once express something like solidarity with this possible response—which I was aware that she, as the host of the evening, might feel unable to articulate, since a direct confrontation with the racist assumptions of the story might lead the conversation into extremely awkward territory, or territory even more awkward than that we were already occupying—and also to be a little bit reticent with my own expressiveness, not wanting to take up the space for outrage to which she would be a good deal more entitled than me, and also, and perhaps overridingly, to hedge my face a bit, in the eventuality that she didn't find his story offensive at all, the lingering possibility that I might overreact 'on behalf' of someone who didn't themselves feel offended made me very embarrassed even in the abstract, so I sat there with one slightly raised eyebrow and an otherwise unreadably confused face listening to this guy, feeling at once like I'd already overstepped the mark and like a total coward, anyway, I don't think he even answered the question about theft, which was soon forgotten (my son woke up from his nap while I was writing this, which means that I've forgotten what I was going to write next, though the irritation I felt at the time of the interruption has dissolved, unexpectedly, into a feeling of indifference or even gratitude, perhaps because I feel really tired from getting up with him five times last night, and in my semi-sleep-like state things are currently arriving into and passing out of my consciousness with the easy fluidity that they have in a dream (as if they are occurring on the other side of a pane of glass, or something) though I confess when he first woke up I recalled C's important item from her list of 'Hateful Things' —*one is just about to be told some interesting piece of news when a baby starts crying*—and then I thought too, as I reinserted his dummy, and rubbed his back, of D, beginning his experience of taking hashish in Marseilles, 'with the absolute certainty, in this city of hundreds of thousands where no-one knows me, of not being disturbed', only to be immediately disturbed 'by a little child crying' (presumably in an adjacent room, or in a room with an open window, across the street, or perhaps somewhere even further away—the noise of a child crying penetrates very far into the world), the sound of which makes 'twenty minutes' feel like 'three quarters of an hour', a temporal disturbance or dilation which anticipates the radical alterations in 'inner experience' which will be revealed to him only a couple of paragraphs later, once the drug has begun to take effect, which made me wonder, as I gave up on the shushing and the patting, if listening to the sound of children crying isn't somehow the inverse of the experience of taking hashish, in the sense that the effects they create are somehow indistinguishable but reached by entirely opposed means, that is, the excessive present-ness enforced upon the listener by the sound of a child's cry has a similar effect of slowing time down generated by the frictionless dissociative state of being stoned, which is maybe to do with the human voice, a sound different from all other sounds in the demands it makes upon and the expectations it creates in a listener, as E suggests, I remember listening very closely and feeling intensely frustrated at the poor quality of the only recording of the voice of my father, whom, as I may have already written, earlier or later, I never knew, and have no memory of, since he died when I was two years old, younger than the age K is as I write, a fact which I find difficult to think about, since I understand how much effort goes into taking care of a baby and a toddler, and how much of this effort is driven by a desire for the love—or the will to care, or something—that lies behind it to be felt by its recipient or object, the child, partly so that they know they are loved or cared for, partly so I know that what I am doing when I care for him has a point (though maybe offering unfelt love, or uncertainly-felt love, would be somehow a 'higher' kind of love, in the way that the feeling of 'friendship' or intimacy I experience with poets who are long dead often feels more intimate than the relationships I have with my contemporaries, since they (the dead poets) can't experience it) and how sad I would be if K and J had no memory of the feeling of that love which I have for them, and which I presume my father had for me, based on the photos I have seen of him holding me, comfortably and intimately, and my mother's sketchy accounts (all of her accounts of anything, any event or memory or person or fact, are 'sketchy', and when I say 'sketchy' I don't just mean that they are restricted to outlines, to vague gestures or broad-brush indicators of intent, I also mean to imply the temporal aspect of the sketch, that is, the sketch as a phase early in the composition, and as such vulnerable to later amendment, which is what has tended to happen with any and all events that occur in her and my life and those of people she has known in the past and hasn't seen in years, that is, their facticity has become, more or less, provisional, a flexible medium for the expression of her feelings in the present moment, since even the most seemingly-innocuous incident (a smile or laugh at the wrong moment, a misheard remark, a misremembered name) can be modulated in some subtle way—because of the analogies with drawing I've been using, I'm picturing

her adding some discreet shading to a portrait
—so that the deviousness or insensitivity or whatever
negative aspect of someone's character can be conclu-
sively inferred from it, an attitude towards the
notion of 'objective truth' that I have been struggling
to acclimatise to, though it is one which perversely
reminds me of my own approach to literary criticism,
which largely consists of often credulity-straining
readings of difficult or abstruse poems, in which
a single word or phrase is made to act as a kind of
prism through which the totality of the often entirely
fictional or confected meaning of the poem can be
perceived, an interpretive approach I now sometimes
think of less as 'imaginative' or 'inventive' and
more as an authorised, focused kind of paranoia)
of his behaviour as a parent, which are nevertheless
convincing enough for me to say confidently that
he did love me and my sister, who I haven't yet mentioned, and spent time and effort and love caring
for us, a possibility which makes me feel ungrateful
for not remembering him at all, or, rather, it makes
me suspect, in a hesitant way, that there is something
fundamentally complacent about my character that
I could be so doted upon, so cared for, and for that
doting and caring to have left no detectable lasting
impression on me, which I know is excessive, nobody
remembers their early years (or some people do,
or at least claim to, I was listening to the radio a few
months ago and an actor was describing his memories of his own birth, and for what it's worth,

I believed him) and I barely have any memories of my childhood at all, up until the age of five or six, when gradually I began retaining scenes with a degree of clarity, not just the features of the external world in which they took place but the invisible texture of my internal experience of them, that is, my feelings and thoughts, some of the clearest of which happen to be memories of fabricating memories of my father, since from the age of five or six teachers and my peers began to ask me about this person, my father, a type of person everybody else (or most people) had as part of their families but which I was lacking, and though it's shameful to admit, I experienced this lack almost as a kind of refinement, a note of difference which distinguished me from the majority, and because I didn't know what a father was, let alone the actual person my father was, I felt no actual absence, I harboured no sensation of loss or grief, it was simply as if, when called upon to talk about this person whom I had apparently spent years in the presence of, I was talking about a hypothetical person, a trace or outline the lineaments of whom I felt barely capable of describing, as when on one occasion my primary school teacher asked me to come and sit with her at her desk while the other children were working, seemingly with the express intention of asking me if I remembered anything about my father, and because I enjoyed being treated in this exceptional manner (I could see some of the other children looking up at me, furtively and enviously, from their own desks) and because she asked me in such a careful and thoughtful manner, I began to fabricate a memory of my father, an image which began to take shape before me, of him standing in a room, warm, crosshatched with slants of afternoon light, through which a vast number of dust motes moved in small, frantic, directionless bursts, as though we were suspended in a glass of fluorescent fizzy drink, where I was sitting on the floor, and he was looking down at me, with an expression on his face which I had copied and pasted from the most benevolent faces in illustrated children's editions of the Bible, and as I was describing this image I remember feeling that these details were sufficient to count as a valuable disclosure, that the teacher should be satisfied, yet the teacher pressed me, ever so gently, to see if there were any further details I could recall, if he (my father) had spoken, or if there were any other noises of any kind, if I could smell anything, was anyone else present, was there any other sensory detail that could flesh out the scene, but I refused to elaborate, a refusal I took a little pleasure in, since the impasse in my memory seemed also to satisfy the teacher in some respect, perhaps even as much or more than a substantially detailed recollection could have done, sensing this I even dramatised my inability a little with some nervous hesitation, as though I were in some way letting the teacher down for being unable or unwilling to bring to light any more memories, suggesting in the process the presence of a psychological blockage of fascinating density which prevented their release, a strange thing to do, I don't know why I didn't just say *no, I don't remember anything, stop asking, leave me alone*, I'm not sure why I was so willing to fake a memory and behave in this false manner just to curry favour with a teacher I liked and to make my peers jealous of the special attention I was receiving, though in some respects this is the one of the less disgraceful falsifications of my childhood (not least, I suppose, because there is a possibility that it is in fact a real memory, and that I have misremembered my invention of it, though I don't really know how that would work or why —in the other tab I have a chapter from *The Science of False Memory* open, which quotes a passage from *Henry V* (Act V, Scene iii) as an illustration of remembering 'with advantages', and now I'm scrolling through an online version of *Shakespeare and Memory*, though my access to the text is limited by the preview function of Google Books, my 'research' methods are amateurish and neither of these partial texts have yielded anything helpful—though I suppose the fact of my being unable to recall any impression or image of my father has been one I haven't questioned at any point in my life, and there might be some sense in which it would be more unsettling for me now to realise that my falsifications of memories were in some instances true, than to go on with the fact of my non-knowledge of him), I was far more elaborate in the accounts I offered to my friends, such as F (whose own biological father was absent—even at the time, the elective absence of live fathers seemed much more serious than my own father's actual existential absence—leaving him to an irritable stepfather who, whenever I visited, I couldn't speak to, since I found him so frightening (itself a reflection of F's own fear), on one instance while we were eating dinner—a bad dinner, I remember, undercooked sausages and cold beans, I remember it vividly (I remember terrible meals more than good ones, like when I think of the elaborate, luxurious or expensive meals I've had during my adult life, usually arranged to mark occasions like birthdays, anniversaries, graduations, and so on, I remember the context much more vividly than the food itself, the theatricality of the occasion, the material abundance, the implicit thread-count of the table cloth, my consciousness of the expense of the meal, a sense of nervousness that the meal would be unable to live up to the staging and the cost and that even if it did that I wouldn't be able to tell anyway, that the playfulness and the elements of surprise and disjunction which are supposed to characterise haute cuisine would be lost on my very lower-middle-class palette (I basically eat in primary colours), that I would nevertheless have to perform enjoyment irrespective of the actual experience of eating, which was maybe not entirely a projection of my own anxieties, there sometimes seems in these kinds of restaurants to be an attempt to cultivate a suspension of critical engagement under the guise of critical attention being heightened, a lulling into acceptance, or a pressure or guarantee not to allow the experience to be unpleasant, which is maybe why I feel relieved when those occasions are over and why I have a kind of blind spot in my memories of these otherwise quite memorable experiences (which are designed, little parenthetical alcoves, for memories to occur in) for the food itself, whereas when I think of unpleasant or disgusting things I've eaten—a lukewarm 'full Irish breakfast' from a tin poured into a cold pancake in a café in Dublin, a slice of underdone cow heart from a street barbecue in La Paz, a burger I had for lunch at school which contained an unchewable string of gristle, the texture of an elastic band (which I remember mainly, I think, because the boy sat opposite me saw me pause in my chewing, and presumably look a bit nauseous, because he looked nervously at me, as though not wanting to know, and said *what is it*), a bun full of roasted pork and apple sauce from a stall at a festival, from which I pulled an incredibly long human hair squeakily through my two front teeth, the metallic, sponge-like texture of kidney in my steak and kidney pie at primary school (while writing this I googled for the sake of comparison 'list of disgusting things i've eaten' which took me to a site which listed ten disgusting foods, the first of which is Casu Marzu, a block of pecorino cheese purposely prepared to become the natural breeding grounds for nests of maggots—'reports are it tastes exactly as you might imagine: strong pecorino, the crawly snot-plump bodies of insect larvae, and the slimy fat they've made of the digested cheese—oh, and the worms jump off the cheese while you're eating it'), a spoonful of dogfood—Chappie with Chicken and Rice, containing Fish and Fish Derivatives (Min 14% White Fish), Cereals (Min 4% Rice), Meat and Animal Derivatives (Min 4% Chicken), Oils and Fats, Herbs, Minerals—scooped out of the meat cylinder in which the threads of the tin had left their impression, eaten as a dare to placate a friend one seemingly endless boring afternoon, one enormous gob of phlegm which emerged into my mouth without my hocking it up, just popped up there, while I was teaching, and which I just had to swallow straight back down—I remember very clearly both the sensation of eating them, which is very close-feeling, very intimate, very ongoing, as well as the mood that the bad experience of eating produced or absorbed, which is a kind of generalised feeling of dissatisfaction and self-disgust, which coloured every other sensory aspect of the moment, as though my body were communicating to me its embarrassment that I was its ward, and that this was the situation I had put us in, and it was trying to pull away from me)—I spilled my cup of juice across the dining table onto his lap and he shouted, probably just to himself or in shock, but I was very frightened of what he might do in retaliation), who one day at lunch asked how my father had died, and since the previous weekend

I had seen an advert on television for a film called *Backdraft* (a 1991 American drama thriller film directed by G and written by I, starring L, M and N, about Chicago firefighters on the trail of a serial arsonist) and which featured several exciting-looking snippets of scenes in which firefighters moved heroically through burning buildings, with one particular scene-fragment sticking in mind, of a flaming ceiling beam crashing down upon one firefighter, resulting in a large amount of grief among the other firefighters and various friends and family of the fallen man, an extreme emotional response which I wanted to appropriate or perhaps allude to, if only for my own benefit, perhaps as a way of registering by antithesis the neutral, even indifferent attitude I held towards my father's blank non-presence in my life, so this became in this instance his manner of death, the burning beam had crushed him while he had been saving me and my family from the house fire, one of several fake deaths my unfortunate father suffered, I remember with some certainty that he also drowned and electrocuted and shot while attempting to prevent a bank robbery, deaths of the kind that I could only have seen on television, violent or unfortunate or meaningful deaths, that is, since everyday death, unspectacular death, the kind of death that most of us will experience, death by heart attack, infection, cancer, organ failure, and so on, is a great deal less visible to us as children, understandably, since if we were confronted with the fact of the probably invisible, slow-moving and ineluctable cause of our demise as frequently as we were with the spectacular or meaningful deaths we were presented with as a matter of routine then the possibility of death would be somehow unthinkable, as X suggests, which makes me think of the TV program I watched with some devotion during that period of my life, *Captain Scarlet* (noun, mid-13c., 'rich cloth' (often, but not necessarily, bright red), from a shortened form of Old French escarlate 'scarlet (color), top-quality fabric' (12c., Modern French écarlate), which, with Medieval Latin scarlatum 'scarlet, cloth of scarlet', Italian scarlatto, Spanish escarlate often is said to be from a Middle Eastern source, but perhaps is rather from a Germanic source akin to Old High German scarlachen, scharlachen (*c.* 1200), from scar 'sheared' + lachen 'cloth', in English as the name of a colour, attested from late 14c., as an adjective from *c.* 1300, Scarlet lady, etc. (Isaiah i.18, Revelations xvii.1–5) is from notion of 'red with shame or indignation', Scarlet fever is from 1670s, so called for its characteristic rash, Scarlet oak, a New World tree, attested from 1590s, Scarlet letter traces to O's story (1850), German Scharlach, Dutch scharlaken show influence of words cognate with English 'lake') in which the eponymous protagonist undergoes a fresh death each week, on each occasion dying in spectacular and meaningful fashion, I have just googled 'captain scarlet deaths' in the hope of coming across a list of these deaths which I can copy and paste here, but have instead come across a fanfic site which features brief flash-fictions describing different, and possibly original (though it's hard to tell) deaths for Captain Scarlet, the list of which runs *quicksand* (the text is superimposed upon a colour picture of Scarlet being pulled downwards into a murky green substance), *the fall* (Scarlet falling backwards from the summit of an extremely tall building, his hat already come loose from his head and somehow preceding him in the descent, heading towards the busy city street below), *cobra* (Scarlet, tied up, pinned back against a tree in a jungle setting, with a cobra, tongue flicking and teeth exposed, centimetres from his anguished face), *thrown from car* (Scarlet looking less mortally afraid than irritated as he falls from the open door of a purple vehicle), *the fuse* (Scarlet, buried beneath substantial rubble, reaches towards a stick of dynamite whose fuse is burning down, but which remains just out of reach), *eaten alive* (Scarlet, weighed down by two large boulders, descends through a green sea, surrounded by sharks), *the spiked room* (Scarlet, his two arms outstretched, palms flat against the spiked walls of a room that has begun to close in on itself, as in one of the *Indiana Jones* films), *crates* (Scarlet looks up, seemingly frozen to the spot, as several large crates fall towards him), *the tank* (a tank pushes Scarlet off a cliff), and *flames* (a burning ceiling beam falls on Scarlet, who falls to the floor), deaths which in their ineffectuality and repetitiousness doubtless informed my own accounts of my father's various dramatic endings, the detail and vividness of which—as I was fabricating these stories (and I'm aware I've written something either earlier or later to similar effect, but I can't find it right now, this sentence has become tediously unwieldy and I am struggling to orientate myself within it, I keep having to control-F certain words or half-remembered phrases in order to teleport myself to specific passages to be elaborated or redacted or whatever) it was as if I could actually see the scenes playing out before me, as though they were not in fact being conceived on the hoof but were somehow being decrypted from some prior bank of imagined narratives, an archive of possibility in which every eventuality is stored, ready to be extracted and played out—makes me realise how under-imagined my father's actual death is, I have hardly any information about it, and what information I do have is from an extremely unreliable source (my mother, who when I spoke to her on the phone today yet again either pretended to or actually did forget the names of both my children, and then became extremely irritated when I objected to this, a response I couldn't resist, or felt obliged to stage, even though it's increasingly clear that she is not herself, there is something so painful about the experience of someone forgetting a name which is important to us that I found myself unable to control my exasperation, my hurt (and I was quite cruel to her, I kept asking her to try to remember, offering her 'five chances to guess it right', giving her 'clues', and so on, and though she initially was able to respond to these aggressive gestures good-humouredly, after a while I began to grind her down, expanding the meaning of her forgetfulness so that it became expressive of more general aspects of her personality, such as the fact that she was a bad parent, that she had never cared about details, that she'd often forgotten to pick me up from school, that she had never bought my children presents and that she couldn't remember what my wife did for a living —it was quite a performance—very wounding, almost arbitrary things, by which, afterwards, when I'd had time to calm down, I found myself surprised) and by the time I eventually told her their names, or, in fact, said 'It's K and J, for fuck's sake', she seemed actually very upset, and, for a moment, before my later regret set in, I did feel satisfied that she had been forced to recognise my feelings through her own feelings being so hurt) though I don't know what it is about that particular kind of forgetfulness that is so intimately wounding, it's not like our names really matter to us, except, perhaps, when we are first meeting people, and when they ask us our name we have to say that name out loud, and with the saying of the name comes the necessity of establishing or retrieving a kind of attitude towards it, which either conveys that there is a degree of continuity between the name and our personality (if we have a very unusual name, for example, and we are lucky enough to have a personality of sufficient uniqueness to realise the promise of the name, in which case presumably the name would be pronounced with the confidence of one who has been truly perceived) or that there's a discrepancy between the two (if we have an outlandish name and a shy or reticent personality, or vice versa, that misrepresentative discrepancy might be experienced as shameful or embarrassing) or even, and I have seen this a couple of times only in very self-assured-seeming people, the attitude conveyed when speaking their own name is one of slight amusement, as though they were not so much being asked their name as being asked to say any random word in the language, as though these self-assured people have never quite overcome the faintly comic arbitrariness of anyone being named anything at all—a rare and irritating type of person—but, beyond this first encounter, our names fade into transparency in the eyes of others and ourselves (even, I hope, the most self-conscious of us), they become merely sounds by which we address others and are to be addressed, by which one of us calls to the other and hopes to receive a response, a gesture that can be oppressive or friendly depending on circumstances, and, as P tells us, nobody who isn't very foolish thinks much about that more-or-less arbitrary connection between ourselves and the sounds or letters which denote us in the social world, or believes that there is a real relationship between the name they are given by their parents and the person they eventually become, which makes it all the more surprising that it should be so wounding when someone should forget a name, or mispronounce a name, or confuse one person's name with another, as if there is an importance to the act of naming each other which only becomes apparent, which only becomes visible, when it's violated—a possibility which makes itself felt in different ways, such as when, as happened this morning, H, after weeks, and perhaps even months of not using my name—during that time she will, instead, use one of the many other nicknames or sobriquets she has for me, which are either private in-jokes particular to us, or common forms of affectionate address, such as *love*, or *baby*, or *darling*, the last of which she pronounces with a bit of a country twang, taking a little pleasure in the cliche, a gesture which sometimes makes the occasionally difficult particulars of our relationship more bearable through their abstraction into more general forms of relation between men and women—our just being one more love to another love—and at others is simply a form of content-less sociability, the lorem ipsum of our days, employed when we are talking about boring things or doing the washing up or whatever, an empty gesture, almost a kind of touch, which is warm and fluid and keeps things ticking on, and, then, occasionally and more intimately, when she calls me by a name used by everyone else used for everyone else, I feel in its blatant and funny inadequacy our own individuation, the particularity of our shared being with each other, unexpressed—will suddenly say it, my name, either in anger or out of love, and I will feel unaccountably and abruptly returned to the scene of myself, as though I was being named again), and these details are so minor and fragmented that it's impossible to piece together a larger scene or sense of the event from them, for example, one of the things my mother told me was that the family dog, R, who was devoted to my father, on the morning of his death refused to go into the bedroom where he was lying in bed, and that when they saw that she refused to enter the room, they (he and my mother) looked at one another in fear, since (according to my mother) they both believed in the intuitive powers of animals to detect in advance the occurrence of some terrible event, there's something both distressing and vaguely comic about this, the obdurate pet who refuses to go into the room to see a dying man, as though she were merely refusing to go for a walk in the rain, I can't bring myself to believe I was physically present as this was happening (which I must have been), it feels strange, but even now, after trying to write about it for a long time, I can't seem to feel anything about it, about someone I never knew, even in the way I care characters in books or on TV shows, though perhaps the closer I get to his age the more I will care, recently I have become more interested in him from a merely practical standpoint, in the sense that over the past year I have been visiting various cardiologists and geneticists in order to work out if he died of a congenital condition that I might have inherited, and which my own children might be susceptible to, so I've been doing a bit of investigating, lying down in a series of darkened rooms with cold goo spread over my chest, as a nurse presses a long white plastic instrument against the middle of my sternum, holding it like a pen, and twitching or shifting it occasionally, as though she were writing something very carefully or hesitantly on my skin, and then with her other hand turning the screen towards me so that I can see the fluorescent pulsing of my own heart, as though she were presenting to me for the first time the image of a foetus, and though it might sound strange I confess I do find it weirdly compelling to see my own heart on display there, beating frantically, there's something oddly recognisable about the messy, haphazard rhythm—determined by a group of pacemaking cells in the sinoatrial node which have the ability to spontaneously produce an electrical impulse (known as action potential, which occurs when the membrane potential of a specific cell location rapidly rises and falls, a depolarisation which then causes adjacent locations to similarly depolarise) generating a current that causes contraction of the heart, travelling through the atrioventricular node and along the conduction system—of it, something I identify with, this squishy thing, it's almost as if my heart seems surprised by each pulse it experiences, as though it had no plan), so after this cringeworthy anecdote of colonialist adventure had been completed, and my pointless vacillations had gone unvoiced, the historian, S, asked me, with a degree of briskness (it was getting late), what my own worst theft was, and, embarrassingly, I couldn't think of anything, even though I had initiated this little game and could have spent the time she and the others had been telling their stories preparing my own anecdote (and here I confess I experienced a small flicker of resentment at how compelling she and even the paedophile-concealing playwright and the fantasist of colonialist adventure had been), smiling in a way that expressed a feeling of puzzlement, I searched my memory for a theft of any kind, I felt my eyes moving from side to side slightly in their sockets, and even though I knew I had stolen many things it was as if, for a moment, I'd never stolen anything at all, I was trying to examine a conscience that was wholly and alarmingly clean, or, rather, it was as if I had returned to the scene of a terrible crime I had committed, with a whole contingent of policemen to whom I had just confessed in exhaustive and tedious detail, only to find all evidence of the supposed crime had been entirely and unexpectedly erased, leading to a charge of wasting police time and a small fine, perhaps it was the circumstances of the dinner that had led my memory to delete its history, or perhaps it was because I was actually too ashamed to confess to the crimes I'd committed, of the things I'd stolen, or perhaps, more likely, I was ashamed of the thrill I was experiencing at the imminent opportunity to expose myself to others, a shame worse than most thefts, as T suggests, and as U elaborates, in his essay 'Confessions (Excuses)'—originally titled 'The Purloined Ribbon'—which discusses in exhaustive detail an episode from V's *Confessions* in which the young author, employed as part of the domestic staff of a wealthy family, steals a ribbon (when I see the word 'purloined' in this context, or any other, in fact, for some reason I find myself thinking of Y, and the way in which the text of *The Pillow Book* first entered circulation in the social world, since by her own account she wrote it purely for herself, jotting down things she had witnessed and the thoughts of her heart while she was away from the palace, at home, with nothing better to do and with no intention that anyone else should see what she had written, and because it might prove an inconvenience in some quarters for her writing to circulate in the social world, she had kept it hidden, she claims, though at the end of her book she offers an account of the moment of its theft, stating that *when the middle captain of the left was still known as governor of Ise* (a city located on the eastern tip of Kii Peninsula, in central Mie Prefecture (formally in Ise Province), on the island of Honshū, facing Ise Bay, a bay located at the mouth of the Kiso Three Rivers between Mie and Aichi Prefectures, which has an average depth of 19.5 metres and a maximum depth of 30 metres toward the centre, the mouth of which is 9 kilometres wide and is connected to the smaller Mikawa Bay by two channels, the Nakayama Channel and the Morosaki

Channel, and is subsequently joined to the Pacific Ocean by the Irako Channel, which ranges from 50 to 100 metres in depth) *he came calling when I was at home, and my book was resting on the mat pulled over for him to sit on* (it is this detail, of course, which makes it impossible, or nearly impossible, to believe that she truly wanted for her book to go unread, for her not to want to have it discovered and exposed, since if she really did want those things she would have kept it more securely hidden, in a box or on a high shelf or maybe just tucked under a pillow or cushion, though, I suppose, if the middle captain of the left did call on her unexpectedly, she may have been surprised while at work on the book, and distracted by the unexpected interruption (and perhaps presuming that the visitor was someone who might only be passing, rather than someone she would invite in) just left the manuscript where it was on the mat, that's plausible, and I suppose too that there's the possibility that she may have felt safe to presume that even if she were to invite a visitor to her house, this person, upon discovering an unidentified manuscript on a mat, would not have stolen it and circulated it in the social world without her permission, so she might not have felt it necessary to go to great lengths to conceal its existence from someone she appears to know fairly well), *but when I quickly tried to grab it* (perhaps it was the very quickness of this gesture which alerted the middle captain of the left to the significance of its contents—I remember one long

Sunday afternoon, as a child, perhaps only six or seven, I had spent the afternoon reading and writing and drawing (the distinctions between these activities had not yet been fully consolidated, I think, I still thought of handwriting—the process of slowly shaping the individual letters with a crayon or coloured pencil or felt-tip pen and concatenating them into words—to be a kind of commonplace, everyday artistic practice, which allowed for an infinite number of variations in style while still remaining basically figurative or intelligible (I never did develop a handwriting style that I could identify as my own, incidentally, when I looked back through my school textbooks recently as I was clearing out my mother's house—which I had sold for her so that she could move into a smaller, warmer, more manageable flat in the middle of a city, close to a shop and a park and various other amenities, and surrounded by neighbours who, if they heard a crash or a bang or the sound of someone crying out for help, would hear and alert the authorities—I saw my handwriting style change dramatically, not just between exercise books (such a development might be expected, over a longer span of time) but from page to page, a shift which, if I recall rightly, was determined by whoever it was that I was sat next to while writing that day, in one entry my hand is joined-up, luxuriously curved, and slightly angled towards the right (as though italicised) which suggests I was sat next to a girl with an ornate, self-delighting hand, and another entry reveals a hard, angular script, entirely written in capitals, the pencil has been pressed into the page with a great degree of force, I clearly remember the boy whose hand that was, the feeling of wanting to try on his idiosyncratic way of doing things, the assertive, singular character of his personality and his writing style, and even today, when I add items to the list on the chalkboard we have in our kitchen —*bean curd, prawns, salted radish, roasted peanuts, beansprouts, chives, basil, minced pork, shiitake mushrooms, coriander*—my writing becomes like H's, which is clear, legible, rounded, and quite large, though sometimes my imitation fails, and I write too large, and H will say that I've taken up too much space on the chalkboard, and I will realise what I've done and that even in my early thirties I've failed to grow out of my childish habit of imitation, and I will find myself rubbing out what I've written and rewriting it in a new style which is not in fact a style at all but merely its negative, a small, scribbled, barely legible script, which makes me feel like a fake citation of myself, which is why I prefer writing on a computer, or at least I think or say I do (it's hard to tell the difference, sometimes), part of me experiences the process of typing out a document as a pleasurable, immediate falling-away of identity, an automatic conferral of anonymity—the text is neutralised of any of the visual kinks or idiosyncratic knots that crab and needle the eye when reading a handwritten letter or essay or exam script (though, of course, any reading experience (but particularly email) is conditioned profoundly by the choice of font, which is in itself highly expressive, in my view certain fonts have a normative, conservative-with-a-small-c character to them (Times New Roman) while others convey a strong impression of literary pretension and even delusion (Garamond, Didot), one or two make me actively groan with irritation (Palatino, Tahoma), and then there is the brisk, administrative non-choice choice of Arial (a sans-serif typeface in the neo-grotesque style—which began in the 1950s with the emergence of the International Typographic Style, or Swiss style, adherents of which looked at the clear lines of Akzidenz Grotesk (1989) as an inspiration to create rational, almost neutral typefaces—designed in 1982 by Z and B, to be metrically identical to the popular font Helvetica, with all character widths identical, so that a document designed in Helvetica could be designed and printed correctly without having to pay for a Helvetica license) which this is being written in, and which I read with or in or through so often it has probably come closest to achieving that sense of material transparency, of un-noticeability, which is the ultimate goal of a certain family of fonts (and of a certain kind of art, what C calls *absorptive art*, that is, a kind of art which allows you the fantasy of the experience of transparency —the airport novel that's so gripping you forget that what you're doing is reading, the film that allows you to forget you're watching a film—or immediacy, achieved by the form's mediation being handled very lightly and indirectly, which is routinely counterposed to *anti-absorptive art*, which often works to achieve those same ends (of transparency and immediacy, that is) but through opposed means, that is, via the foregrounding of process, material, artifice, and so on, the seams that are so disgusting, and these two approaches to achieving similar or identical goals are often charged with opposed political characters, too, naturally the airport novel is the reactionary aesthetic choice of the bourgeois businessman, and the disruptive, difficult, writerly text is the choice of the revolutionary, though I don't believe any of that—but as I'm writing I'm remembering that there's that documentary about fonts, isn't there, or just about Helvetica, I think, which I've never used, and which makes me think, since I have thought so little about this subject and have nothing original to contribute, that I should close this window) and what's attractive about that is that I'm able to indulge in the fantasy that what I am writing has, in fact, been written by someone else, and that I am reading it back to myself as a critical reader, which is of course impossible, A, the illusory suspension of identification between myself and text lasts only a few seconds while my brain takes in and adjusts to the new visual field, the blind spot I have for myself and my own writing re-establishes itself, the hole out of which and towards which I write), and for whatever reason I found myself writing out a series of hypothetical statements of feeling, in a range of cartoonish fonts, such as 'I wish I was a hundred', 'I am bored bored bored', and 'my favourite food is fish fingers' (it wasn't), and, then, for some reason, 'I hate my mum, I wish she was dead', a statement which, as soon as I saw it written before me, produced in me a strong feeling of dread, as though simply by writing it the statement had passed from the realm of the hypothetical or speculative or experimental into that of actuality—since I had written it, it must in fact be, in some sense, true—which is why when my mother came into the room as I was looking at this thing that I had written, in a peculiarly upbeat-looking font (bubble-letters filled with multicoloured dots), I snatched it away from the table and placed it into my lap, a gesture which obviously drew my mother's attention, I regretted it immediately, the obviousness of the movement to conceal and obscure or deceive, *what's that*, she said, not in an accusatory fashion, but curiously, and perhaps even a little apprehensively (I have experienced that feeling myself as a parent, that faint sense of apprehension, when I have seen my children hiding things from me and I have said those words, *what is it that you're hiding there*, I will say, *what is it*) and when I handed it over to her and saw her read what was written there and her expression fall away I felt my face flood with shame (the colour not just red but *scarlet*, and I said it inside, as though tracing the letters, *scarlet*)—perhaps if she had reached for it slowly and nonchalantly then he would not have found the manuscript so interesting that he felt himself compelled to steal it) *he got ahold of it and took it away, and returned it to me only after quite a long time, and it was after that that it began to make the rounds*) from the bedroom of his employer, and when the entire staff is lined up and confronted about the theft, I does not just not confess, he in fact blurts out the name of the maid with whom he is in love, D, I think, who as a result of this lie loses her job and has her reputation seriously damaged, a peculiar thing to do to anyone (though of course there might be a reason, or a few reasons, intelligible only to the person making the decision and never available to the rest of us, for why we might lie) let alone someone you love, and it's the strangeness or apparent unintelligibility of the act which seems to interest E, in this weird and beautiful and chilling essay, which offers a number of different interpretations of his blurting out of the name G and the subsequent confession(s) of the crime, which I unfolds with a virtuosic fluency which seems so effortless it has a whiff of contempt about it, particularly in his first interpretation, which reads the utterance of the name L in light of M's conception of love, articulated elsewhere in his oeuvre, based, more or less, on the principle that love should be exactly reciprocal, that the other, the beloved one—in this case, N—should return the love of the young O to such a degree of equivalence that the two figures within the relationship become, essentially, substitutable for one another, variables within an equation, and as such become responsible for one another's actions, which is to say that since the young I stole the ribbon with the intention of giving it to his beloved, P, then, more or less, R is already complicit in the action of stealing, and should be prepared to suffer the consequences, an account of the incident which —despite it seeming to me an audaciously imaginative version of the young S's motivations—T clearly finds contemptible in its simplicity, in its merely psychological conception of motive and action, a feeling which is less detectable in the subsequent interpretations, the most notorious of which is that I merely blurts out U not for complex psychological reasons but because it was the first thing that entered his head, he said it at random, he 'excused himself upon it', in that peculiar syntactical formulation, because V was on the tip of his tongue, and that in fact the calamity of this situation, and the terrible consequences that befall the maid with whom I was in love, are not really attributable to his blurting out of the word W at all, but rather to the falsely referential reading of the random utterance, the tendency of the social world to forget the fictiveness of language, and so on, which I won't go into, since what I and everyone else vaguely familiar with this essay will be sure to point out is that it has been read as a veiled or cloaked or otherwise disguised defence of X's own collaborationist activity in Belgium during the Second World War), and it was with a sense of mounting panic nearly at its peak—even at this moment of crisis I can't recall thinking even in passing of my real lie, my real theft, my real claim that I had remained in the kettle at the protest, had stayed in the plural pronoun, secured in the historical moment that all other moments were squandered in the service of, when I had, in fact, scarpered—that I finally recalled an incident that I had told once before when someone had asked me this same question some time far in the past, or something like it, someone who I may have been trying to impress for some reason, I can't think why else I would have chosen to tell it since it is a boring story but one from which I emerge with my character not entirely soiled, or so I thought, it was in fact this earlier telling of the story, which took place at a time and in a place the details of which I can't recall (though the impression of striving very hard to impress whoever this invisible interlocutor was is intensely vivid to me even now, A, as is so often the case I can only recall the texture of the experience rather than its particulars, the syntax of it rather than the content) rather than the actual incidents it described, that I was recalling as I told it, the essence being that there was an unattended squash racket leaning against a fence on a street near my childhood home (I was maybe thirteen or fourteen, I had, perhaps, just started reading *Middlemarch*), I was walking past it with my friend, my best friend at the time, Y, whom other people (his parents, my mother) thought was always leading me astray, we would smoke and drink and occasionally watch porn together, the television muted, on opposite sides of a dark room (on one occasion he even took me into his parents' bedroom and took out from the bedside table a sheaf of porn magazines and a giant dildo, I'd never seen anything like it, and after several minutes of intense reading (though I wonder if it's correct to classify the act of looking at images as 'reading') he, seeing the state of arousal that I was in, invited me to use his bathroom to masturbate), he wanted to steal the squash racket, I said no, not because I didn't want it (it was a Slazenger, pretty new, the sleeve for the racket-head was a glossy green, bright and untarnished) but because I think I was afraid of being caught, we were in public, by a main road, cars streaming by at what would now seem an unbelievable speed, what if someone saw, we had a quite heated exchange about it, me not just resisting the theft for myself but trying to persuade him not to take it, him calling me a chicken, this being part of a larger pattern of persuasion and resistance between us that made our parents' essentially correct intuitions about our dynamic all the more intolerable, and I eventually won, though the experience of winning was deflating, since it was a case of my cowardice triumphing over his daring, we began to move away from the squash racket, only to be called back by the head of a middle-aged man which had just appeared from above the fence the racket was leaning against, the owner of the squash racket, it turned out, who wanted to congratulate me on the quality of my character and condemn my friend for his moral turpitude, we looked at one another, my best friend and I, and I could not interpret the expression on his face, for it was maybe a distance from expressiveness which was visible there, a withdrawing of his interiority from view, and it was as if, for a second or two, he were no longer a person but merely an object displaying the external properties of personhood, a machine (1540s, 'structure of any kind', from Middle French machine 'device, contrivance', from Latin machina 'machine, engine, military machine; device, trick; instrument' (source also of Spanish maquina, Italian macchina), from Greek makhana, Doric variant of Attic mēkhanē 'device', from PIE *magh-ana- 'that which enables', from root *magh- 'to be able, have power', main modern sense of 'device made of moving parts for applying mechanical power' (1670s) probably grew out of mid-17c. senses of 'apparatus, appliance' and 'military siege-tower', it gradually came to be applied to an apparatus that works without the strength or skill of the workman, from 17c.–19c. also 'a vehicle; a stage- or mail-coach; a ship', and, from 1901, 'a motor-car', also in late 19c. slang the word was used for both 'penis' and 'vagina', one of the few so honoured, the political sense 'a strict organization of the working members of a political party to secure a predominating influence for themselves and their associates' is US slang, attested by 1876, Machine age, a time notable for the extensive use of mechanical devices, is attested by 1882, though there is this—'the idea of remodelling society at public meetings is one of the least reasonable which ever entered the mind of an agitator: and the notion that the relations of the sexes can be re-arranged and finally disposed of by preamble and resolution, is one of the latest, as it should have been the last, vagary of a machine age' ['The Literary World', Nov. 1, 1851], Machine for living (in), 'house', translates Z's machine *à habiter* (1923)), a boring or at least uneventful story and one that in this instance I had to alter slightly for effect, though the particulars of the alteration that took place on this occasion are now lost on me, I could sense that my dining companions were a little disappointed after the vivid and affecting opening admission of theft and the subsequent scandalous and inflaming stories, and I didn't fully listen to anything else that was said for a long time, in the slowly emptying room, and though I was very relieved that my turn was gone, I kept thinking about what I'd said, and because I was absorbed in thinking about it I became so quiet that I probably seemed rude, or bored, perhaps annoyed that my story hadn't gone down well, I hardly said anything for the next couple of hours, I couldn't tell you what was said or done, what passed between us, and I was thinking about this again earlier today, this tendency to zone out in the presence of other people, for the feeling of parentheses to open up inside me even as others are speaking, even as I am being directly addressed, and for me to begin to elaborate some kind of imaginative doodle (a list of names or objects which is then subjected to some kind of arbitrary organisational principle—girlfriends in order of birth date, cities in the world I would like to live in, my worst mistakes in order of badness, films I have watched while high, crimes I feel capable of, and so on—in this childish interior space over which I feel I have complete autonomy, until, that is, I realise however faintly that the primary situation of *being addressed* is still ongoing and continues to reach me, at an admittedly low volume and subject to some kind of slowing effect —the words reach me at a reduced pace, and with a kind of blurring treatment applied to them, so that they have become a sustained noise comprehensible only at a very general level, with only occasional striations of intelligibility, usually in the form of names, since it seems like names are the elements of speech which are the last to fade into the background, even when I'm feeling at my most distracted as someone is speaking there is still operative an automated form of attention capable of registering proper names as they are mentioned, somehow raised into relief above the background of what is spoken, so that it's possible, even when I have not been listening in any substantial way, if I am brought back into the present company of other people through a direct question, for me to use these names as a series of co-ordinates from which the terrain covered by this speech or conversation might be speculatively plotted, since there are only so many vectors around which a group of familiar names congregate, I know that if I hear B and C in close proximity then the subject is likely to be D, if I hear E, F, and G, the subject is almost certainly I, this latter subject, in fact, represented a particularly good possibility at the time during which this conversation took place, since almost every subject could, it seemed, be brought round to I, as the underlying subject from which every other subject seemed only to momentarily depart, or towards which every other subject seemed to gravitate, almost as if we, by which I mean virtually everyone I spoke to for several years, were in love or in horror of it, much in the way that, during any life, there are periods in which there will be certain people with whom every aspect of the world seems suddenly involved, towards which every detail of the world seems to refer—and that this is shaping the operations of this thought-bubble, and as soon as I recognise that I realise I have to open up an interior within this interior, for further protection, at which point the initial situation from which I have abstracted myself seems tolerably far away now, and the prospect of returning to it seems so unlikely that it's almost relaxing, having immobilised myself in this nested space, as I mentioned I was thinking about this today, during an argument with my mother, something which happens too frequently—my becoming distracted during arguments, that is, rather than arguing with her, though that, too, occurs too frequently, especially in recent months, and despite my changing awareness of her mental state I still find myself layering my attention, abstracting myself from my conversation with a differently abstracted person, like, in many ways, the fathers of the friends I had during my childhood, many of whom seemed to me unpredictable and occasionally volatile beings, who were only rarely physically present when I visited my friends' houses but, when they were physically present, often seemed not just not present but several layers removed from the rooms they were in, and were nevertheless somehow much more present in their absence, a presence detectable in the palpable sense of freedom with which we played when the fathers weren't there, we would be particularly loud when playing football in the garden, or run around the house at dangerous speeds, chasing one another and shrieking, or indulge—in the case of my friend L—in games which had an explicitly 'feminised' streak, such as our practice of looking after a large group of L's soft toys, for the purposes of which we would find ourselves speaking in girlish or sometimes babyish voices, pretending we were each other's mothers, each other's children, cuddling and stroking the toys and each other, a game we became careful not to play when L's father was around, since, one afternoon, after school, he had overheard us playing in this way, and entered L's room with an unusual urgency—we'd heard him coming loudly along the corridor, and looked at one another, sensing that something was about to go wrong—and shouted, with an anger that I'd never witnessed in my life, that we should *stop talking like girls*, this phrase lingered after he left the room, as though imprinted on the air, I remember the sound of it even now, and I also recall the echoes of it which I experienced afterwards, especially during those periods of my childhood when I would endure a particularly severe bout of flu, for some reason this would always result in hallucinations of such vividness and clarity that the atmosphere of them remains with me today, I was always alone, at night, lost in a large and empty city, the dark buildings of which stretched up so far into the sky as to indicate that the conventional physical laws of the world were being flouted, they even seemed to sway a little indolently, these buildings, like strands of vegetation or the tentacles of a jellyfish moved by a current of water, and I was being pursued by a figure, largely indistinct but certainly male, whom I never saw—and indeed I'm not even sure if the figure was ever actually embodied in any recognisable sense—but who I was aware of as a sound of extraordinary volume, a sound which I wasn't in fact hearing, but which I was perceiving in a generalised way, as a kind of energy which was straining at the limits which had been placed upon it and which was the only threshold keeping it from reaching and, I was fairly sure, harming me, on one occasion, I was perhaps seven or eight, this was happening to me in such a vivid and lifelike fashion I locked myself in the bathroom of our house, and I recall my mother was on the other side of the door, trying to reach me, pleading with me to open the door, and her pleas were very painful (late 13c., 'punishment', especially for a crime, also 'condition one feels when hurt, opposite of pleasure', from Old French peine 'difficulty, woe, suffering, punishment, Hell's torments' (11c.), from Latin poena 'punishment, penalty, retribution, indemnification' (in Late Latin also 'torment, hardship, suffering') from Greek poine 'retribution, penalty, quit-money for spilled blood', from PIE *kwei- 'to pay, atone, compensate' (see penal), the earliest sense in English survives in the phrase on pain of death) for me to hear since it was clear that she was a spy for the figure or amorphous malevolent energy that was pursuing me, and that she was using everything in her power, every trick in the book, in order to deceive me and hand me over to this presence, the fact of my mother's duplicity struck me then with the force of a revelation and cast a chilling pall over the events of my life up to that point, all the acts of love and tenderness, the happiness, the play, had been merely preparation for the final betrayal which this moment represented, and as I stood on the toilet, the seat so cold against the soles of my feet that it seemed, in fact, like a kind of heat, I think I knew or intuited some overlap between the sound that I thought of myself as being pursued by and the voice of L's father, an unfair connection to draw, and one which was less about the actual character of L's father or the particulars of his actions than the fact that I had very little contact with men until the age of eleven, when I began to be taught by them, at school, with greater frequency, and they became a normalised presence in my life, but up until that point I'd known very few men, all my teachers were women, and my mother never introduced any of her boyfriends to us, doubtless in an attempt to protect us from the disruption that a man would have on our family dynamic, though now I think of it a man did come for Christmas once, a man called M, the nature of whose relationship with my mother I'm still uncertain of, since the way she spoke of him was with a kind of mixture of pity and irony that makes it seem unlikely that he was a boyfriend, or perhaps not, anyway he came for Christmas at our house, I was maybe nine or ten, and he behaved in a way that confirmed my developing view that men were strange and unpredictable creatures, he smelled strange, he was wearing an outfit entirely made of denim, he would drink the clear fluid straight from the bottle he had brought with him, and when we played a game of snooker on the miniature table that I'd been given for Christmas he suggested that we bet on it, a bet of something like fifty pence, the idea of which I was delighted by since I don't think I'd ever bet on anything before, I might not have even understood what gambling was (one of our few family myths or legends is that my maternal grandfather, who spent much of his career as a newspaper journalist in Berlin and Bristol, invented the game known as 'spot the ball', which was a frequent feature in British newspapers for several decades, the substance of which is that a reader or player of this game has to guess and pinpoint the position of a ball which has been removed from a photograph of a moment from a football match, to identify (usually by marking the image with a cross) the location from which this object—towards which the jostling players in the photograph continue to strive, usually in bodily positions suggesting extreme stress or animation, and with expressions on their faces of determination or intent, as if they were chasing or being chased by a ghost—has been been extracted, and which may be classed as betting, a prize competition, or a lottery, depending on its form) and I was horrified to discover the true nature of the arrangement when I was defeated at snooker and M began to demand his winnings, at first jovially, then with what I took to be increasing seriousness, and I didn't know what to say, I didn't have any money, I was a child, which was something I wanted to say to him but which I knew would elicit contempt, *I'm a child*, having to tell someone who or what you are is embarrassing, why isn't it self-evident, but he kept on about it, the fifty pence, until my mother said something like *Oh for god's sake, M*, and the exchange ended abruptly, and, though he stopped talking about it, I remember being looked at by M and thinking that the feelings expressed towards me by that look were emphatically negative, though I couldn't be sure, this was what unnerved me about him, and about men in general,

I couldn't tell what they were thinking, or they seemed to be thinking murky or dark thoughts I didn't have a language for, and that when they in fact revealed what they had been thinking it was usually something negative, a vague feeling of irritation or hostility the sum impression of which was the understanding that I was being wished out of existence) a process I was trying to describe to H the other night, as we were having a drink outside—it was the last night of the month-long heatwave, when even Scotland was warm enough to be uncomfortable, a period which led even N-owned newspapers to speculate whether global warming was in fact real—and because we were speaking in an open and relaxed fashion (for my part, probably because I was aware that our neighbours could hear us talking—all, or most, of the windows of the tenement were open —I was maybe more measured in my own assertions and receptive to accounts of my mother's behaviour, and my own responses to it, than I am in the private space of our own home, or I was certainly speaking differently, more sympathetically, even to myself, in a way I can't fully define, sometimes I think that all of my problems could be solved by my being deceived into thinking that I am constantly being overheard, which I suspect may in future lead me to convert to some religion or other governed by a surveilling deity, or to accept some new technology, which can hardly be far away, in which all my (all our) speech is recorded by my iPhone or future equivalent, so that there can be no doubt about the factual content of events, like goal-line technology in football, which would not only remove the doubt from many situations in which something criminal happens, but could actually be used in resolving day-to-day arguments, these arguments my mother and I have, for example, when they have reached their sixth or seventh 'movement', tend to double back on themselves and take as their subject not the originating issue or dispute, but the way in which the other person engaged with that issue or problem, a phase in which mutual misrepresentation of earlier stages of the argument becomes rife, a situation in which a transcript of the unfolding argument—perhaps projected onto the wall—would be helpful, though of course many of these later-stage movements focus not so much upon what is actually said (in terms of 'words spoken') but the inflection or tone of those words, the unarticulated energy behind them, accurately determining which would be something beyond even the most sensitive recording equipment, I imagine, since more often than not we don't actually understand or hear the tone in which we're saying something, especially when we're trying to defend ourselves, when we feel like we're under attack and nobody else is there to defend us so we have to defend ourselves, though of course after time has passed and the argument has collapsed and the pressures and energies which drove it in its earlier phases have wholly dissipated and dispersed, we realise that the urge to defend ourselves not only undoes our attempts at self-defence, not only prolongs our own pain, but equips our foe (who is also our ally) with a new repertoire of examples by which the basic flaws of our character can be illustrated) we were able to talk about this idea that I was no longer actually speaking to my mother in such instances—*that she is in fact no longer there*—a passage I tried and failed to write during the strikes I mentioned earlier, or will mention later, which I felt OK about, since it was a period during which I thought I should probably stop work of all kinds anyway, including on this sentence (as I've taken to calling this essay or zuihitsu or novel or email or monologue or text—*what is it*—that I started writing to you, A, but which now seems to have turned away from that opening impulse, become distracted into something else, and which I've been keeping a secret, though unexpectedly the other day, at the picket, with J and K in the double buggy, eating their second helping of free doughnuts, absolutely covered in sugar,—they were very much at home—I did tell a friend, O, that I had been working on it, and explained briefly and awkwardly the governing principle that, as P resolved to write her zuihitsu only until the paper she'd been given by the Empress ran out, I was just writing it until I reached fifty thousand words—or, later, when it became apparent that the constraint had been overspilled by the content, or that this initial constraint was tied to an external condition (by which I mean a fact of reality) which during the composition changed, the governing limit became 100 pages, though it later reverted to the fifty thousand rule—at which point I would stop, which she said she thought was a good idea, at least in the abstract, though as I was describing it to her, O, who is a novelist and whose approval I was seeking—she is a good judge of an idea in my experience, she assumes an attitude of reserved skepticism when encountering new information, and seems genuinely reluctant to indulge in the niceties of social etiquette, which makes her a valuable sounding board on aesthetic questions even if it means I don't actually enjoy her company very much, in the sense that she doesn't offer me a uniformly or even predominantly pleasant experience when I speak to her, she says things that make me feel uncomfortable without any visible discomfort on her part, she sometimes interprets some things I say in ways that make me understand them in new, often difficult-to-process ways, or makes me understand that they are communicative of meanings I didn't intend when I said them, which is alarming, the sensation, that is, that I am being spoken through by impulses beyond my comprehension—as I was describing it to her I began to feel like either the idea for the text was better than the text itself, or the idea was interestingly bad in a way the actual thing could never be (this tossing looks *harmonious from a distance, like sea or the tops of trees, only when one gets closer is its sadness small and appreciable*, as R puts it) and then later on, pushing the buggy back across the Meadows, and feeling a little nauseous from the doughnuts, as I was recalling what she had said and how I had talked about it to her, trying to detect in the manner of my description of it if it was my intention to carry on writing it, for some reason I thought of the phrase 'impossible buildings' as a kind of analogy to the kind of impossible-seeming writing exercise I'd embarked upon (though, of course, if I'd been better-informed at the time I started writing it I would have known that this exercise wasn't at all impossible, as it has already been done by S in his *Dancing Lessons for the Advanced in Age*, an almost perfectly measured single sentence which in my edition (the Vintage translation, by T) is 100 pages of text, though it also features lithographs by U, so that length obviously couldn't have been one of the original principles underlying the composition of the book, the actual length of which I've no idea about (in word count terms) and of course V himself probably wouldn't have known at the time of its composition, since the word-count as a measure of length only really came into use after the advent of the electronic word processor (unless you counted each word by eye or hand or finger, which seems unlikely), which is probably what would have enabled the poet and artist W to write her first book, *Dies: A Sentence*, which consists of a single, fifty-thousand-word sentence, which I haven't read and probably won't read, since the idea of reading a fifty-thousand-word sentence written by someone else seems pretty gruelling, and also because I guess I'm a little concerned to discover that *Dies* is a more rewarding reading experience than this, whatever that means, or because I am afraid of coming to realise in the experience of reading it that X was having a better time writing it than I am having writing this, as though the sentence were a unit of experience which could return to you in vivid form the character of your being in the world, in all its richness or paucity) and wondered if anyone had had the idea of designing some (impossible buildings), which, of course, someone has, when I googled the phrase I came across the website of the Catalan, Barcelona-based artist and photographer Y, of whom I'd never heard, but who has created, through a combination of photography and 3D digital rendering, a series of hyper-realistic images of buildings which it would be physically impossible to build in our world ('The techniques I use are often described as "camera matching" or "perspective matching" and several 3D software packages provide functionalities that allow you to perform this', he explained, but added that he tends to add do a lot of the work by hand to 'reach the level of detail needed to achieve high photorealism'), at least at the moment, with engineering at its current state of development (who knows, perhaps in forty years' time some new material will have been discovered that will allow such structures to exist), buildings like the oddly-titled 'Defence', which consists of a thin, shabby-looking building which rises vertically about five floors, then from which a much larger block juts out horizontally to the left for dozens of 'floors' (though presumably 'floors' would be 'walls' in that horizontal arrangement), a structure which in reality would, of course, be fatally unbalanced, a lesson which I have been trying to impart to K, when we play with his Duplo, and after a usually quite promising beginning to the process of constructing a tower—a few blocks will clump together to form a rough base, and then an erratic-looking vertebrae, constituted of horribly clashing colours, will start developing upwards out of it, and becoming almost immediately unstable—it will collapse unspectacularly, limply toppling, causing him to cry and become confused and frustrated and angry, feelings which I will try to assuage or mollify by explaining that this event can be prevented from occurring again (or can be made to occur much less frequently) by approaching the task of construction in a more considered and systematic fashion, and as I'm trying to explain this I will also be demonstrating physically how this should be done, first creating a solid, wide, square base, and then building a narrower tower on top of that (look, I say, watch) lacing together into a sturdy object those bricks with six nodules or little circles on top so that forces which will shortly test the integrity of the structure (gravity, a child's finger) will have a greater chance of being absorbed or resisted by being distributed among the seams which both connect and divide the individual blocks, though as I explain this to him he refuses to be comforted, if anything my explanation makes him even more distressed and he begins to wail, which I find difficult to deal with because by this point I have become authentically absorbed in the task of assembling the tower, the activity has become wholly detached from the occasion or the need which gave rise to it, much in the way a poet, in an era long before our own entry into the world, would receive a stipend or a commission from a patron, and in agreeing to receive this fee the poet would commit themselves to paying tribute to the patron in some way in the artwork which the fee enabled (by clearing time for the poet to write poems rather than, presumably, just being destitute or having another job, such as barman, cook, scribe, or clerk, or lawyer, and so on, all of which activities would have diminished the amount of time for the poet to spend thinking about poetic things, though of course the activity of working in a field unrelated to poetry might itself prove equally if not more generative of poetry, depending on the sensibility of the poet), usually through a dedication at the front of the work, in which the patron would sometimes be addressed directly and praised lavishly for their beneficence, their accomplishments in the political world, the nobility of their family, their splendid house, and so on, and though many of these dedications or addresses to patrons are formulaic, and rehearse familiar tropes and employ routine image-sets, others, such as those by Z, are obviously ironic, using these familiar tropes in such an exaggerated or histrionic manner that it becomes clear that the poet is lampooning the obligation to gratitude and subservience the poet-patron relationship has enforced upon them, though perhaps most interestingly there are occasional examples in which it becomes apparent, some distance into the dedicatory passage, that despite (or maybe because of) the murky or troubling or unstable circumstances of its composition the poet has become authentically absorbed in the activity of composing, so much so that a degree of imaginative detachment from the originating impulse for the work (whether accepted as a necessary part of the economy of poetic composition, or implicitly rejected as a 'corruption' or distortion of the artistic process, which presumably should occur as naturally as leaves to the tree) has been achieved, and that this originating context (or the pretence of one) has in fact entirely evaporated, or has become so obscured by the manoeuvrings of the poet's syntax, which have taken the poet so far into the poem (as though into the labyrinth, from which there seems no escape until it has been escaped) that they cannot see how it began and how it will end, though of course this is merely an unverifiable response I have experienced when reading such poems, and in fact I can imagine how the verisimilitude of the depiction of authentic absorption in the artistic act enabled by a financial transaction which is swiftly transcended might itself represent the most fawning of possible tributes (so gracious and enabling is the patron that they themselves have facilitated their own marginalisation in favour of the foregrounding of the artwork, and so on), especially since even in such instances it's at no point entirely clear who is speaking, the poet or the patron (is the former simply a mouthpiece for the latter, or the latter a platform for the former, and so on), or who is looking over whose shoulder —*who is looking over my shoulder*—or in what unstable compound these two figures or entities speak through one another, which is a predicament expressed almost constantly today in realms far beyond the act of poetic composition, such as on social media, where it seems that anyone who has a connection to an institution of any kind (or is employed in any capacity) supplies a caveat in their bio note stating that 'all views are my own' (when I see this phrase I tend to think of something my mother once said, when talking about an old boyfriend of hers from college, I think, who was a PHD student, and when I asked what a PHD was—I was maybe nine or ten at the time, though to be totally honest I didn't really know what a PHD was until my early twenties—she said that it was a qualification that you received when you contributed an 'original thought' to the world, a nice definition, I think, but one which she delivered to me in a tone which conveyed an unstable compound of awe and contempt, as though she were so overwhelmed by the profundity of the idea of an original thought that she was suspicious of anyone who claimed to have had one (immediately after offering this definition, she said, 'I've never had an original thought in my life', again with an odd combination of resignation and delight, as though the inability to think anything original were a cause for both despair and celebration), an attitude which I must have absorbed in some distorted form, since shortly after that conversation I discovered the page on Ceefax (a text transmission system developed in the late 1960s by engineers at the BBC, originally intended to transmit a printable page of text during the nocturnal 'close-down' period of normal television transmission, but which rapidly developed into a sophisticated electronic 'site' operated with the remote control, which I used to watch live updates of football scores on, the experiential analogy that first sprang to mind on the first day I used the internet, that day so long ago) dedicated to the compilation of inspiring or insightful quotations or epigrams from philosophers and writers from throughout human history, and which I soon began dropping into conversation with my mother, without any kind of preamble or the slightest concern for their relevance to the conversation at hand, as though it were completely natural for a child of nine or ten to say *you know, mother, luck is what happens when preparation meets opportunity,* or *when I let go of what I am, I become what I might be*) a phrase which seems, oddly, to be both wholly untenable and a kind of humblebrag, in the sense that when a person asserts the expression of their 'own views' in a given situation, the inverse—the scene in which others' views are expressed by the mouthpiece of the person—becomes sharply imaginable, and it makes me wonder, perhaps unfairly, if there is some overlap between those who assert the own-ness of their own views within the private or social sphere (as social media presumably is, or was) and the kind of person I have encountered many times in my life, who when in 'work mode' takes a visible and almost perverse pleasure in acting as a transparent medium for the intentions of the institution they represent, like the traffic warden who, once he has started issuing a ticket, states with an expression that conveys an odd mixture of resignation and pleasure that there's nothing I can do, an attitude which is probably in part related to or drawn from or generated by the relief of not having to choose how to act (so many of us hate having to choose, especially when the choice has consequences in the real world, when it effects the experiences of others and knocks their lives off the course they would otherwise have taken, it's a terrible thing, in a way, the freedom to select between the few options placed in front of us (for there are always only a few options, one to five, even though in theory it seems like the options are limitless), between giving a ticket or not giving a ticket, between two people we are involved with and who we love and are loved by and who offer to us two different lives to take up and put down, between two homes or two jobs, between the few recipes we know how to cook for dinner, an abundance of narrative possibilities so abstract and rich and fertile-seeming that it's almost paralysing, so much so in fact that sometimes we would rather choose *not choosing* above making a choice—*no, I don't want it, take it away, it's tainted, I couldn't*—and the way we rationalise this withdrawal from choice is to believe that not choosing were somehow the ethical or responsible route to take, as though it were better to deny our own agency and let the 'fates' or the constellations or the I-Ching or the SatNav decide or for events to run their course and so on, rather than to take responsibility for the task, which confronts us hundreds of times every day, of choosing between possible presents and possible pasts and possible futures, fully in the knowledge that once each choice has been made it will not just alter irrevocably our lives and the lives of those who are entangled with our own, but that that moment will stay there, and part of us with it—the version of us that made the choice and experienced it—fixed and suspended in an ongoing present, forever, as B hypothesises, an unbearable pressure of responsibility which is perhaps the reason why we like to play at choosing, or I do, at least, some of my most pleasurable evenings in recent months have just been spent 'trying to choose' a film to watch on Netflix or Amazon Prime and failing to come to a decision, since in the very act of shuffling through the seemingly-infinite range of choices available, in postponing the act of decision-making, I have found myself experiencing something closer to the aesthetic experience I'm after than any experience offered to me by any actual film, which is, of course, an endless deferral of closure, an infinite postponement of the resolution of form, but as well as enjoying the postponement of decision when I'm in very similar if not exactly identical mood I also like to play at actually deciding, which is the activity offered by the Moral Machine, a website hosted and operated by a research group at MIT whose purpose is to develop through crowd-sourcing a picture of a general moral system to determine how self-driving cars should behave in moments of potentially fatal uncertainty, a site which offers a vast number of different traffic scenarios in a basic cartoonish simulation and asks the user to decide which figures to save and which to plough into—a man and a woman are both walking across zebra crossings, a baby in a pram and three cats are crossing a road, a pregnant woman and two young workers are crossing one side of the road and on the other is a roadblock which would surely kill the passenger of the self-driving car, and so on—and collates these human responses in order to develop a picture of what is considered a proper or at least intelligible moral response when these narrative possibilities arise in real life, in the coming future which cannot be very far away or perhaps has even arrived in some parts of the world already, in Silicon Valley, presumably (I should confess at this point that I don't actually know if Silicon Valley is a 'real' place or not, is it just a marketing phrase for an area that's not even a valley or is it really a valley, it's one of those places that I think I would be surprised to find out if it was the latter) in which self-driving cars have entered the bloodstream of our highways and our backroads and our existing moral universe, this game of choosing is, like all voting, pitched ideally in terms of maintaining an individual's psychic equilibrium between inconsequentiality and consequentiality, in the sense that there remains the flickering possibility that the decision I input into the simulation will inform how a self-driving car in a San Francisco street in twenty years' time will steer, but that the decision is so infinitesimally small and insignificant in the larger scheme of assertions that I can assuage any anxieties I have about the rightness or correctness of my own intervention by persuading myself that it represents merely a dot in a pattern, a flake in a flurry, a pixel in the image of a culture, though I have reservations about this project, and not just about the traffic-scenario-simulation itself, since I find it hard to see how by offering a series of choices which have to be taken for the simulation to proceed, it can accurately account for the tendency of humans in times of crisis not to decide, simply not to act, to abstain, to postpone recognition of the severity of the moment until the very fire touched them, as C writes, when, describing the Great Fire in 1666, he offers a scene in which people and animals behave in a fashion which has little to do with an intelligible moral system, 'everybody endeavouring to remove their goods, and flinging into the river or bringing them into lighters that lay off', and 'poor people staying in their houses as long as till the very fire touched them, and then running into boats, or clambering from one pair of stairs by the waterside to another', and, perhaps most weirdly and movingly, 'among other things, the poor pigeons, I perceive, were loth to leave their houses, but hovered about the windows and balconies, till they some of them burned their wings and fell down') but also, and perhaps more alarmingly, communicates the idea that this complete abdication of agency—*there's nothing I can do*—is an authentication of the importance of the institution (the local council, usually) to which the warden has subordinated his own will, an authentication which verifies the justness of his decision to subordinate his will to the institution in the first place—though this willingness to subordinate the will to the command or the advice of an external figure or force can also be turned against the person who has agreed to go along with what they've been told, after the event, if things have gone badly or even disastrously, and it turns out the command or advice was misjudged or miscalculated, when the very willingness of others to be instructed, to be acted through, is used as an excuse or exculpation by the external figure or force, *of course we should be listened to in all circumstances*, it will say, *except in circumstances when it becomes obvious that we should not be, in which case common sense should be employed,* and if in such instances common sense—a strange, amorphous, virtual, conditional and shifting form of knowledge, to be activated at some imprecise juncture during the unfolding of an event—is not employed, then the decision of those who continued to follow the instructions as instructed is presented as an error of judgement, a turning point, at which salutary civic-mindedness becomes uncritical biddability, a change which occurs immediately, without any interval, *there is hardly a moment in between and it is really too bad very much too bad naturally*—since, after all, it is important enough for it to have stripped him of his agency, a loopingly self-justifying erasure of the self in service of the institution or whatever impelling agency I also encountered during the protests I wrote about above or below, I forget, on the faces of the policemen who stood in a long line in front of the protesting students and walked towards them slowly and inexpressively) which is, like all of the writing I do and which my colleagues at universities do, potentially subject to a retrospective reclassification, that is, though I feel like I'm writing this for pleasure, right now, on the 16th of May at exactly noon (and as if to prove this to myself I've decided to look out of the window for a while at the tenement flats opposite and list what I can see, though I can't actually see anything beyond the brick walls of the buildings and the glass of the windows themselves, since the sun is shining on the windows and the interiors are so dark as to be invisible), with the children out with their mother, my legs crossed in a relaxed fashion beneath the table, the radio in the kitchen faintly audible, it is pleasure I'm experiencing, I'm enjoying the process of writing in a loose and definitely leisurely way, but I can foresee the possibility that it might become 'work' at some point in the future, if it were to be published, and submitted for the Research Excellence Framework exercise (a process of expert review, undertaken by the four UK higher education bodies (the Higher Education Funding Council for England (HEFCE), the Scottish Funding Council (SFS), the Higher Education Funding Council for Wales (HEFCW), and the Department for the Economy, Northern Ireland (DFE)), and carried out by expert panels for each of the subject-based units of assessment (UOAS) (Clinical Medicine, Public Health, Health Services and Primary Care, Allied Health Professions, Dentistry, Nursing and Pharmacy, Psychology, Psychiatry and Neuroscience, Biological Sciences, Agriculture, Veterinary and Food Science, Earth Systems and Environmental Sciences, Chemistry, Physics, Mathematical Sciences, Computer Science and Informatics, Engineering, Architecture, Built Environment and Planning, Geography and Environmental Studies, Archaeology, Economics and Econometrics, Business and Management Studies, Law, Politics and International Studies, Social Work and Social Policy, Sociology, Anthropology and Development Studies, Education, Sport and Exercise Studies, Leisure and Tourism, Area Studies, Modern Languages and

Linguistics, English Language and Literature, History, Classics, Philosophy, Theology and Religious Studies, Art and Design, History, Practice and Theory, Music, Drama, Dance, Performing Arts, Film and Screen Studies, Communication, Cultural and Media Studies, Library and Information Management) under the guidelines of four main panels (Health and life sciences, Physical sciences, engineering and mathematics, Social sciences, Arts and humanities), to secure the continuation of a world-class, dynamic and responsive research base across the full academic spectrum within UK higher education, achieved through the threefold purpose of the REF (to provide accountability for public investment in research and produce evidence of the benefits of this investment, to provide benchmarking information and establish repetitional yardsticks, for use within the HE sector and for public information, and to inform the selective allocation of funding for research)), in seven years' time as one of my *key publications*, to which I would probably have to ascribe a number (on a scale of 1–4) to indicate its quality, whether it is of international significance, or of merely local significance, an embarrassing and impossible process I have just been through with a book of criticism and a book of poems I spent the last five years working on, which in the self-assessment exercise I rated as 4* publications, that is, 'of international significance', a judgement based on nothing which, if ratified by the panel members, who will be reading several dozen comparable works in a short period of time, presumably will mean that the department I work for will receive more research funding for a defined interval before the next REF exercise, to allow for further volumes of international significance to be produced, and so on, and the fact that this retrospective classification of leisure as work can take place means that, even if it actually doesn't happen, everything I do —brushing my teeth, shitting, eating my lunch—is inflected by the knowledge that it contains the possibility of becoming work, which means that even just by sitting at home, writing this, I feel myself suspended in a state of what D calls, semi-convincingly, *pre-commodification* (as I was writing this K, who is back from the shop and now doing a PJ Masks puzzle, said, quietly, and without looking up, 'your work is very boring') and am, as such, undermining the strike, a possibility I'm not sure what to do with, since the logical conclusion of this feeling is, I guess, for strike conditions to be observed immaculately, time itself has to be arrested altogether, the pause button pressed on life, until all of its elements can be reconfigured, and since this is impossible in actuality, A, the options seem, at this moment, to be to despairingly concede that all life is somehow complicit with its own demise, or to act as though time could somehow be made to behave in a fashion which made this impossible dream visible, a vague feeling I was trying to explain to my mother this morning, while on the phone—she loves the fact that I, that we, are on strike,

A, not just because she was a teacher, or because she has always been a union member, but because I can call her up in the middle of the working day, and when she asks what I'm doing, and I say *fuck all*, she laughs and says *me neither*—sat in my new, slightly nicer middle-class apartment in a central area of Edinburgh, feeling lazy and full of reheated stew and fruit crumble—I allow myself a little indulgence when H is at work and I'm at home with J, who is currently in her brother's room, I can hear her pulling jigsaw puzzles off the shelf, singing to herself a continuous song without words, a song made of noises that cannot be written, the alphabet having no letters that can syllable the sounds, as E writes of the nightingale in the orchard in Northborough—toggling between this document and three news sites, waiting for something to happen with I, suspended in this condition of contentless anticipation, waiting for something to happen for so long I've rotated through my set structure of phases (indifference, irritation, irony, annoyance, concern, exhaustion) an incalculable number of times, though I have noticed not without pleasure the phenomenon of that structure of repetitions coming to feel collective in texture, over the past few months, in the sense that there are only a limited number of responses to any particular set of events, and many people have occupied or been occupied by most of these responses at one point or another over the past two years (a few days before Christmas H and I were invited to dinner by a couple of friends, N and P, both of them poets, who have just moved up the road and were having a party to celebrate their new flat, which was large and beautiful in the way Edinburgh tenement flats can be, with unnecessarily high ceilings and pristine, polished-wood floors, and even though it was last-minute we were able to get a babysitter for that evening, so we decided to go, a little overexcited from the spontaneity of the whole enterprise—H and I don't go out very much any more, and when we do we sometimes don't seem to know what to do with ourselves, the transition from the staged chaos of our family life, in which several conversations and noises and activities are constantly overlapping, braided together in a way that is sometimes deeply stressful and sometimes pleasurable (in the sense that this complex, extemporised process of braiding or folding—work overlapping with play with domestic chore with conversation with planning and recollection and presentness, as though I had too many tabs open—means that virtually nothing gets done or finally completed, it can take me a week to paint a wall, the process of washing and folding and putting away clothes seems a literally endless task, and it sometimes seems as if the process of preparing then cleaning up after a meal has not yet been completed before the preparation of a new meal has already to begin, a feeling of constant motion —of the present making an incessant series of demands on our attention, *like a gate that has never stopped opening*, as R puts it, in her novel which is not a novel but its negative image, a novel written in the seams of the novel form—which can, when I stop and think about it, be completely immobilising, can leave me lying on the floor staring at my phone, watching my inbox silently fill with administrative tasks I will postpone indefinitely, with my children playing and dancing around me, refreshing the same three news sites not in order to gain any information, but simply for the feeling of *having refreshed*, but this same set of circumstances can also mean, when I am in a different mood, that there is a sense of durability to activities that, were they not being constantly interrupted or impeded by the cries or yells of one or the other of our children, or something being dropped or one of our phones ringing or emitting one of its range of alert tones, would immediately dissolve into the past, forgotten or obliterated as moments of non-being, empty time, the lorem ipsum of experience, and the very difficulty of completing any task in our current situation, like reading upside down, prolongs and particularises our experiences, stretches them across, or, in fact, over several days (the activity of living in this way sometimes feels spherical, like we are collectively inflating a balloon, the surface of which thins as it increases in area) in a way that, when we are happy, and when our life is good and pleasurable, is a formal principle I cannot imagine living without, though our children are growing and I can already feel the encroachment of its conclusion) to a space of privacy, of uninterrupted conversation, is almost too abrupt, we find ourselves slightly stunned by the aftershock of having stepped out of our element—and when we arrived we found our overexcitement met no resistance, the dinner was already underway (we were late), there were a few unexpected additional friends there who we hadn't seen in a long time, and everyone had already had some wine, so after we had eaten (we assembled our own tacos from a range of delicious vegetarian fillings that S had made, and which had been arranged on the wooden kitchen countertop) and drunk too much wine (the following morning—looking from the living room doorway at the clothes strewn across our sofa, where we'd had sex as soon as we got home from the party—H and I discussed whether we had in fact gotten too drunk, and made fools of ourselves (*I was definitely shouting at one point*, H said, murkily, *but happily, I think*), I distinctly remembered saying some things which as I said them I knew I would later come to view with some regret or suspicion, like telling one of the slightly younger poets there that he should *just get on with writing poems* in a brusque way that I intended to be encouraging but came out as dismissive, as though I didn't care about his legitimate concerns or doubts about the act of writing and how it relates to the rest of his life, his political beliefs and so on, even though later that same evening I found myself talking to T, an older poet who I have known for several years, about my own writing (and my slightly exaggerated anxieties about it and how and whether to finish it and whether to send it to anyone, and how, it came out, I'd in fact already sent it to O, a mutual friend, who'd responded that it needed some plot or some kind of framing device in order to licence the digressions, some semblance of familiarity or generic structure in which a dissociation of meaning could be achieved through a form that was itself not spectacularly disorganised, good advice which I responded to by quoting U—*don't think this all doesn't nauseate me, even I find it so tiresome that it makes me impatient*—then found myself resisting partly on principle and partly out of laziness (while wondering if I couldn't somehow formulate laziness into a principle without the disorganisation of the text becoming simply a projection of my disorganisation in life, which makes me wonder sometimes if the aesthetic of 'difficulty'—which I talk about all the time with my students, as I'm making them read poems upside down—isn't designed to elicit the ideal kind of 'writerly' engagement with texts that V conceives of, but is simply another expression of a refusal to do the hard work of organisation, the emotional labour of making it—*what is it*—cohere, and thereby delegating that labour to the reader) since it would require a wholesale restructuring of the entire text, and at this stage even the most minor amendment or addition to it has become an extremely time-consuming activity, since when I modify even a single letter or a comma the whole mobile body of the text has to adjust itself, which, admittedly, when I am feeling out of ideas or memories and just want to pass some time by looking at this document—sometimes I zoom out very far, so that the text becomes illegible (or only legible in a very general sense), and look at the narrow column of four fully-populated pages—which is the maximum that can be viewed at any one time in the screen display—then gradually zoom in until certain words become sharp enough to identify, then when I realise that the block of text has particularised itself into this form, I experience a momentary desire to press delete—is an odd and not unentertaining performance to watch, making the text twitch and self-adjust by giving it a little poke) and who seemed enthusiastic about the compositional principle, despite which I found myself soliciting some more substantial approval, and receiving some brusque *get on with it* advice of the kind I'd literally just given, but, nevertheless, feeling wounded and being a bit standoffish afterwards (*I'm sure it's fine*, H called, a little wearily, from behind the bathroom door) sometimes I find myself physically wincing when I recall how I've behaved the night before, and I turn my head away from whatever direction I've been facing in order to physically force a change in my thoughts, or I close my eyes or sharply breathe in as though to not see or to somehow obscure the sound of my own (soundless) recollection, there are particular memories I have which are now decades old yet still produce this response with as much freshness and intensity as those which only occurred days ago (when I was a boy, maybe eight or nine, I was charged with looking after my class's collection of eggs for half an hour or so after school had ended, the three or four eggs were bedded in a little cage filled with straw or some straw-like substance beneath a weak heat-lamp, I remember looking at them for some indeterminate period of time not just in the hope but in the expectation that they would hatch under my gaze, which didn't happen, and which was quite frustrating and boring, but more importantly I remember very clearly when my mother came to pick me up that the teacher, who had been supervising my supervision of the eggs, told my mother in a generous and humorous fashion that I had been a *very good mother*, in response to which I said, in a kind of bitchy tone, *at least someone has one*, for no apparent reason, or for no reason I can now recollect, and the look of hurt on my mother's face is vivid and clear to me now, as is the silence in which we drove home, I really don't know why I said it, it was as if it was almost an automated response generated by the teacher's remark and the presence of my mother, though of course there's no reason why my remark should have been such a negative one, I could have said something sweet like *hey, I learned from the best*, or whatever, but no, I said my shitty thing and whenever I think of it it makes me close my eyes and turn away, the way I tell people who ask about my first experience of trying to write a poem that my first composition was produced at primary school, was entitled 'Bad Boy', and the first few lines of it ran, *my mummy says I'm a bad boy, / she says that's why she hits me*, another falsification which in this instance did in fact lead to some official inquiries into my mother's parenting and which, again, I don't understand the provenance of as a gesture, when I thought of this today I decided to call her, my mother, for the first time in months, we haven't been speaking since she forgot my son's birthday, which has been a stressful period, not least because it's been difficult to know whether or not she's aware of the fact that we haven't been talking, since during the normal periods of communication between us I would call her every few days or so and yet sometimes, when she would pick up the phone, it was as if she was hearing from me for the first time in years, as if I had been to the Arctic on a scientific expedition or had returned from the southern tip of Patagonia, such was the surprise and enthusiasm with which she would greet me, a warping of personal or psychic time which means that this gesture of silence I have undertaken, this principled stand, may not have even been registered by the person it was intended to rebuke, but whether or not she noticed the period of time that had elapsed since our last conversation, or if there was another reason I do not and will not understand, she picked up the phone today, and simply said, *no, not now*, and hung up the phone, and that phrase has been lingering over the past few hours, naming that feeling of invisibility, of strandedness, that arises when someone refuses to recognise or share in the temporality we hope to be our own (like the fabric that is only noticed when it rips, as W puts it, in his 'Attempt to Exhaust a Place in Paris', or is it 'An Attempt at Exhausting a Place in Paris'—it is only when temporalities diverge, or one asserts itself over another, or one fades away or becomes obsolete or is overthrown for whatever reason, that the idea of shared time shows itself to us in all its importance, as X writes, Y *quotes reports that during the Paris Commune, in all corners of the city of Paris there were people shooting at the clocks on the towers of the churches, palaces and so on, thereby consciously or half-consciously expressing the need that somehow time had to be arrested, that at least the prevailing, the established time continuum had to be suspended, and that a new time has to begin,* an imperfect and nicely ajar paraphrase of the light and assertive passage in Z about *the melodramatic rupture revolution actualises between temporalities and the societies they arrange and authorise*, a process perhaps merely more condensed than actually distinct from other historical processes of time-change, such as the phasing out of traditional Japanese timekeeping with the introduction of European hours after the arrival of Christianity in Japan in the 16th century (the first instance of this change comes in the form of a clock gifted from U, a Spanish Society of Jesus saint and missionary, to B, a *daimyō* (powerful Japanese feudal lords who, until their decline in the early Meiji period—an era which extended from October 23, 1868, to July 30, 1912, and which represents the first half of the Empire of Japan, during which Japanese society moved from being an isolated feudal society to a Westernised form—ruled most of Japan from their vast, hereditary land holdings) of the Sengoku period, in 1551) up until which point water clocks (or *rōkoku*, literally 'leaking' + 'cutting, measuring') had been the dominant mode of timekeeping, though it was introduced in a staggered form, in the sense that the technology of European mechanical clocks was initially introduced in order to measure and accommodate the uneven traditional Japanese temporal hour system—these timekeeping practices required the use of unequal time units, six daytime units from local sunrise to local sunset, and six night-time units from sunset to sunrise (the typical clock had six numbered hours from nine to four, which counted backwards from noon until midnight, though the hour numbers one, two and three were not used in Japan because these numbers of strokes were used by Buddhists to call to prayer) and as such, Japanese timekeepers varied with the seasons, the daylight hours were longer in summer and shorter in winter, with the opposite at night—before a later stage of development, in which the two temporal systems were only partially integrated, which led to the production of some extraordinary mechanisms, such as the Myriad year clock, (or the Ten-Thousand Year Self-Ringing Bell), a universal clock with seven different indexes of time's passage, including both Western solar time and Japanese lunar time, invented by C, a Japanese rangaku scholar, engineer and inventor who in 1875 set up a company, Tanaka Seisakusho (Tanaka Engineering Works), the first manufacturer of telegraph equipment in Japan, which after his death changed its name to Shibaura Engineering Works, and in 1939 merged with Tokyo Denki to become Tokyo Shibaura Denki, more commonly known today as Toshiba—the company which made the laptop I am currently writing on—until, in 1873, the Japanese government adopted Western style timekeeping practices, including equal hours that do not vary with the seasons, and the Gregorian calendar) as I have done so often, when I have said to my mother, no, now is not the time, no, not now, I cannot see you, I am not ahead or you behind or you ahead and I behind, no one is ahead of his time, it is only that the particular variety of creating his time is the one that his contemporaries who also are creating their own time refuse to accept, and they refuse to accept it for a very simple reason and that is that they do not have to accept it for any reason, we are in different histories, parallel streams) the conversation, or the conversations—for by this point in the evening, as always happens when a party goes well and everyone is a little drunk, you end up having only fragments of conversations, which are always interrupted by other conversations, and everything is left pleasurably and alarmingly unfinished—between the ten or twelve or however many people were there by that point, almost inevitably turned to I, and there was something both comforting and unsettling about the resemblances between our states, or the series of related states which we had passed through, the central shared characteristic of which seemed to be a strange centring of concerns upon the present, concomitant with the blocking or the foreclosing of the possibility of the future (though perhaps I wanted to see this too much, perhaps it was merely a projection, this desire for congruence or parallelism, perhaps I simply imagined it all) a negative community D describes as developing most frequently in the aftermath of a disaster, which results in the suspension of certain social norms, a disclosure of partial freedom in how we behave towards one another —I remember when the mother of a boy at our school died, people who didn't even know the boy—myself included—let alone his dead mother, wept openly and at length, even appeared to take (and, in my case, actually did take) a perverse or merely logical pleasure in comforting one another in our unfounded and therefore possibly illegitimate sorrows, there was almost something more touching about the fact that we had no real reason to be sad, to be crying in the library and in the classroom, the seeming illogic of it made our sadness somehow more potent or palpable (to ourselves at least)—but it's as if the event which brings about this collective experience of feeling has been slowed down to such a speed that the 'progressions' or 'shifts' hardly register, like that E piece, *As Slow As Possible*, which will be 'played' by an organ in Halberstadt, Germany (a town in the German state of Saxony-Anhalt, the capital of Harz district, located north of the Harz mountain range, and known for its old town centre that was severely damaged in World War II—in the last days of the conflict, in April 1945, US forces approached Halberstadt as they attacked remaining Nazi troops in the short-lived Harz pocket, dropped leaflets instructing Halberstadt's Nazi ruler to fly a white flag on the town hall as a token of surrender, and when no white flag was raised, on April 8, 1945, 218 Flying Fortresses of the 8th Air Force, accompanied by 239 escort fighters, dropped 595 tons of bombs on the centre of Halberstadt, killing about 2,500 people and converting most of the old town into some 1.5 million cubic metres of rubble, which American troops briefly occupied three days later) for the next 622 years (assuming, that is, that the organ, the church, Halberstadt, and Germany, as they roughly stand at the moment, continue to exist for that long), and which has been playing the same note (the 13th in the piece so far) since October 5, 2013, and will continue to play this note until September 5, 2020, or, rather, that because the phases of response I mention above or below have had the time to rotate so frequently and with increasing centripetal speed during the prolonged period of the event's happening, they have begun to 'blur' as they rotate, so that what in fact started out as a number of discrete moods or feelings have blended into a neutral, liquid band, a transparent sphere, though this morning, Monday 14th January 2019, 9.56, sat in my car typing this quietly while K sleeps in the back, parked up by the Meadows, I am wondering if it might be ending, might be beginning to end, this feeling of interminable delay, this contentless anticipation, this deferral of resolution, this resistance to closure, since tomorrow (the term already dated) the vote on G's deal will happen, and if that fails, as it surely will, then L will call for a vote of no confidence in the government in the hope of triggering a general election, and if that fails, as it surely will, then that will open up the possibility of Labour throwing its support behind a second referendum, and if that fails, I don't know what will happen, which is alarming since it seems like in order for anyone to know how to decide what to do tomorrow they should know what will happen after tomorrow, or any of the other eventualities which might transpire should anything happen, but if it succeeds, and the decision to leave is reverse or revoked, what will happen to this time, this interval in which other futures presented themselves vividly, is cancelled or forgotten or lost forever, though I suppose it, too, did happen, will have happened, though it will be obscured, its particulars erased or simply blurred out, a possibility I was thinking about as I went out this afternoon, in the bright winter sun, to just walk around the Meadows, which I haven't done in months, and only did today because for the first time both our children were at nursery, and H was at work, so I had a whole day to myself, which in the context of the past two years in which I have been writing this sentence for you, A—wasn't it odd, incidentally, or maybe just unnerving, to be addressed last night by N, as part of the collective pronoun 'you', and to be told that she is on 'your'—that is, 'our'—side, a use of the collective pronoun which, while immediately generative of a feeling of claustrophobia or enclosure, also offered, as though simultaneously or somehow adjacent to this initial feeling, a perverse flicker of hope that I, that a 'we', was being truly addressed, a moment of enormous importance which only a handful of words later has been displaced and virtually forgotten, since P has long since resigned and we are stranded in this suddenly advancing day —seems now an outsize, gigantically spherical period of time, too large for one person to fill, so with nothing in mind except filling this time I walked out of my front door, east across the grass, in the direction of Arthur's Seat, a hill formed by an extinct volcano system of Carboniferous age (lava samples have been dated at 341 to 335 million years old), which was eroded by a glacier moving from west to east during the Quaternary (approximately the last two million years), exposing rocky crags to the west and leaving a tail of material swept to the east, listening to R play the piano in 1955, the year my mother was born —as I wrote in the notes section of my phone, which because of the brightness of the daylight was obscured by a too-clear reflection of my own face on the screen, which—I could see this with distressing clarity—has become over the past few years crosshatched with lines and wrinkles, is puffier than it used to be, but also, from this unusual angle, looking down at my own reflected face as though from above, also reminded me of several different people at once, several people whom I couldn't identify exactly or distinguish from one another, but who seemed to be momentarily revealed as I turned my features this way and that, in the extreme, almost hygienic morning light, as though this face were itself a set of anonymous citations even it did not understand (in his account of reading in bed, or, rather, his account of the thousands of books that surround his massive bed ('probably bigger than Napoleon's', he boasts) and cover much of its surface, and of the pleasure he takes in reading while surrounded and nearly submerged by these objects, S contrasts the pleasurable, leisurely activity of reading in bed (which he characterises as an essentially 'French' approach to reading—by which suggestion he of course brings to mind the work of T, whose famous novel, which I've not read, opens with a rich description of physical indolence, of reading idly in bed in the early evening, during which the substance of the book that he had been reading comes to populate, in mildly distorted form, the dreams that take place after he falls asleep) with the characteristically 'Eastern' physical convention for reading, that is, sitting formally at a desk, which is where he does his writing, he writes, during which activity, he reports, he has been informed that his face takes on a 'frightful and forbidding expression', one which he has held or sustained for such long periods (he has written many long books) that the vertical lines which have formed between his eyebrows, the visible seams or striations of his feeling, will never go away, a fact which seems to surprise him, since the expression on his face and the trace it has left in his features don't appear to him to be representative of his interior life as he experiences it while writing, a slightly uncanny disconnect with which I sympathise, since, as H has told me many times, my face will tend to take on a frightful and forbidding expression when I am at my happiest or most enthusiastic, an unsettling thing to live with, I imagine)—and then did a loop back towards our flat, through alternating patches of sunlight and shadow (where the grass remained glassily crunchy underfoot) where perhaps because of the brightness of the sun and the crispness of the shadow it cast and because I wasn't yet hungry I decided to stop at the sundial at the west end of the Meadows and, after passing a few minutes in a kind of semi-willed trance, imagining the open grass filled with two dimensional cartoon players, started to read the plaque, which I'd never done before, and which informed me that this, the Prince Albert Sundial, was one of few remaining pieces of evidence of the International

Exhibition of Industry, Science and Art which took place in Edinburgh in 1886, and that the sundial marked the entrance to the exhibition buildings themselves, which were constituted of a permanent 'Great Pavilion'—which, the designers suggested, because it would be built using steel roof beams and cast-iron supporting pillars and an exterior of rendered brick, glass and corrugated iron, 'may be easily removed to another site (much in the way U, when describing his hut near the capital, stated that *since I was not much concerned about where I lived, I did not construct the house to fit the site, but simply set up a foundation, put up a bit of a roof and fastened each joint with a metal catch, so that if I didn't care for one place I could easily move to another—just how much trouble would it be to rebuild, after all?*) and can be altered to suit almost any possible purpose, without interfering with the general construction'—behind which a range of temporary timber structures were to be erected for the duration of the exhibition, a total of 102,000 square feet of exhibition space for a dazzling array of exhibits, including four full-length locomotive trains placed on 250 feet of railway track, a four-tier linoleum ziggurat erected by the prominent department store Cranston & Elliot, 'which, like a veritable Tower of Babel, overtops all the rest and reaches almost to the skylight', violins from Prague, six working bakeries, vast displays of pickles and preserves, the replica of the Doowoon, an advanced river cruiser built by William Denny & Brothers for the

Irrawaddy Flotilla Company, Turkish embroidery and a Women's Industries display which exhibited Belgian glove making, Fair Isle, Shetland and Icelandic knitting, three hundred pieces of embroidery by Indian women, the Free Church of Scotland's display of artefacts from the Livingstonia Mission—a foundation central to the Scottish evangelising project in the Nyasa region of southern Africa—including an assegais barbed so as to make it almost impossible to withdraw them from a wound, a mock-up of a typical house, demonstrating some of the latest technological conveniences for the home, displays of consumer merchandise such as that of Palmer of Princes Street, exhibiting 'Japanese, Chinese, and other Foreign Goods', a reconstruction of Netherbow Port as it would have been in the 17th century, the Hamilton joiner V's inlaid table of 250,000 pieces of wood, (which represents 'an immense amount of labour, and is a speaking testimony of extraordinary application, patience and perseverance'), and, at the centre of the Artisan Court, The Grand Obelisk Trophy of the Brassfounders of Edinburgh, a thirteen-foot column embellished not only with all the emblems of the trade, but with shields of twenty Scottish Royal burghs and the national arms of England, Scotland and Ireland, and crowned by an idealised figure, a worker who, as W tells us, was 'attired in classical tunic, stands with thoughtful, intent face, surveying, it may be presumed, the work on which he is engaged', despite which seeming abundance and variety, some commentators, having become so refined in their tastes by the scale and ambition of international exhibitions in the late Victorian era, were unsatisfied, with one claiming that 'while the Liverpool Exhibition was widely international, as beseemed a great maritime city, that of Edinburgh was so in little more than the name, scarcely, indeed, even British, but acutely provincial—in too many respects, indeed, almost parochial—alike in conception and execution', and while I was thinking that J and K would have loved to have gone to that exhibition, or just to have walked around the buildings which are not there, I found it strange in a familiar way, wondering, almost without curiosity, if I was going to tell about the bits that were missing, the dropped thread, the distant clause, the parts which had happened before or after now, so I decided to share a photo of the open common beyond the sundial, which is so flat you can see almost all the way across its mile-long breadth, registering that in its place once stood these buildings populated so richly by this diverse array of objects, of which no real trace remained, except this small monument, inscribed with the names of masons and the crests of noble families and of regions, and, on the pedestal below the crown of the sundial itself, a selection of well-known quotations on the subject of time—I MARK / BUT THE HOURS / OF SUNSHINE, WELL ARRANGED TIME / IS THE SUREST SIGN / OF A / WELL ARRANGED MIND, MAN'S DAYS / ARE

AS A SHADOW / THAT PASSETH AWAY, and so on—which, because I had nothing better to do, and for the pleasure of it, and since I thought it might interest you, A, I thought I would write down.

Acknowledgements

This book was written with and through many other texts, to all of which I am grateful. These are only a few of them:

Sei Shōnagon, *The Pillow Book*; Yoshida Kenkō, *Essays in Idleness*; Kamo no Chōmei, *Hojiki* (all trans. Meredith McKinney); Samuel Pepys's diary; George Eliot, *Middlemarch*; Walter Pater, *The Renaissance*; Gertrude Stein, 'Composition as Explanation'; Walter Benjamin, *Illuminations* (trans. Harry Zohn); Clarice Lispector, *The Passion According to G.H.* (trans. Idea Novey) and *Agua Viva* (trans. Stefan Tobler); George Perec, *An Attempt at Exhausting a Place in Paris* (trans. Marc Lowenthal); Bohumil Hrabal, *Dancing Lesson for the Advanced in Age* (trans. Michael Henry Heim); Theodore Adorno, 'Lyric Poetry and Society' (trans. Bruce Mayo); Paul de Man, *Allegories of Reading*; John Ashbery, *Collected Poems 1956–1987*; Denise Riley, *Impersonal Passion: Language as Affect*; Vanessa Place, *Dies: A Sentence;* George Wilson Smith, 'Displaying Edinburgh in 1886: The International Exhibition of Industry, Science and Art'; *The Land We Saw, the Times We Knew: An Anthology of Zuihitsu from Early Modern Japan,* ed. Gerald Groemer; *The Columbia Anthology of Japanese Essays*, ed. Steven Carter.

( ) (   ) p   prototype
poetry / prose / interdisciplinary projects / anthologies

Creating new possibilities in the publishing of fiction and poetry
through a flexible, interdisciplinary approach and the production of
unique and beautiful books.

Prototype is an independent publisher working across genres
and disciplines, committed to discovering and sharing work that
exists outside the mainstream.
    Each publication is unique in its form and presentation, and the
aesthetic of each object is considered critical to its production.
    Prototype strives to increase audiences for experimental writing,
as the home for writers and artists whose work requires
a creative vision not offered by mainstream literary publishers.

In its current, evolving form, Prototype consists of 4 strands
of publications:
    (type 1 – poetry)
    (type 2 – prose)
    (type 3 – interdisciplinary projects)
    (type 4 – anthologies) including an annual anthology
    of new work, *PROTOTYPE*.

Lorem Ipsum by Oli Hazzard
Published by Prototype in 2021

The right of Oli Hazzard to be identified as author of this work has been asserted in accordance with Section 77 of the UK Copyright, Designs and Patents Act 1988.

Copyright © Oli Hazzard 2021
All rights reserved

No part of this publication may be reproduced, stored in a retrieval system, or transmitted, in any form or by any means, electronic, mechanical, photocopying, recording or otherwise, without the prior permission of the publishers. A CIP record for this book is available from the British Library.

Design by Traven T. Croves
(Matthew Stuart & Andrew Walsh-Lister)
Cover detail from illustration 'Bletchley #140' by Catrin Morgan
Typeset in Minion Pro
Printed in Lithuania by KOPA

ISBN 978-1-913513-09-2

( ) (   )   p   prototype

(type 2 – prose)
www.prototypepublishing.co.uk
@prototypepubs

prototype publishing
71 oriel road
london e9 5sg
uk

( )

This is an advance reading copy only